Praise for *Heart Like an Ocean*

From page one, Christine Steendam had me hooked and caring about what happened to Senona, a character that I could identify with even though we are separated by centuries. Christine does an awesome job of showing how human emotion and desire flows as one across the expanse of time ... and oceans. I don't want to give any spoilers, but rest assured that you'll feel the roll of every tide right along with Senona and the ending is not one that you'll be able to guess! Can't wait for more from this awesome author!
– Sara Barnard Bestselling author of *An Everlasting Heart* series

The romance is fraught with conflicts which made me want to tear my hair out at times or melt when the passions ignited.
I rate Heart Like an Ocean 5/5 stars. Recommended for readers who love historical epic tales with a rich cultural backdrop and a mature romance that will tug at your heart strings.
Looking forward to reading more from this author and glad I made this purchase
– Anne-Rae Vasquez author of *Doubt: Among Us*

I didn't consider myself a historical romance reader- but this book has proven that I simply didn't give the genre a chance. I'm definitely a fan! Eloquent and passionate- this book is a must read.0
– C. Elizabeth Vescio author of *Uncontrollably Wasted*

I will be looking out for more books by this author and look forward to her next offering with excitement!
– Lisa J Hobman Bestselling author of *Bridge Over the Atlantic*

I highly recommend this book- it has action, adventure, great characters and, much like it's main character, exceeds the limits of what it's been labelled; this book isn't a good historical romance novel, it is a GREAT BOOK.
– Andrew Lorenz Creator of *Legacy* and *New Guard.*

Praise for *Unforgiving Plains*

This is a great book! Get your pajamas on, grab your favorite blanket, get a diet coke and curl up in your favorite chair and enjoy this sweet book.
-Stephanie Lasley, from The Kindle Book Review

It is a great book to curl up with on a cold night with a cup of cocoa to escape into a beautifully portrayed landscape with characters that you will root for…or possibly, thump on the forehead.
– CaSondra Poulson author of *Calling Me Home*

Romance and building suspense come together to make Unforgiving Plains a very enjoyable contemporary western. Ms. Steendam has a writing style that is easy to read. I would recommend this book to readers of romantic suspense and contemporary westerns.
–Denise Moncrief author of *Crisis of Identity*

Overall, a wonderful story, plausible, heartfelt and with endings that bring you back to earth gently.
– Barb Fenwick

Christine Steendam is clearly a very versatile writer and the shift from historical to contemporary romance was done effortlessly. I would certainly like to read more contemporary romances from this author.
-Lisa J Hobman bestselling author of *The Girl Before Eve*

There is a depth and richness to each character that makes them come alive on the page. I am keeping my fingers crossed for at least two more books. Please!
– Patricia Grimaud

This is tale worth reading, as readers enjoy the push and pull of opposites against the beauty of the great white north!
– Ind'tale Magazine

Owned by the Ocean

CHRISTINE STEENDAM

Hazelridge Press
Box 21 Group 37 RR3
Dugald, MB
R0E 0K0 Canada

ISBN 13: 978-0993925917
ISBN: 10: 099392591X
Owned by the Ocean
Christine Steendam
Copyright Christine Steendam 2014
Published by Hazelridge Press

Cover Design: Frisson Design
Author Photo: Prairie and Pine Studio

First Edition/First Printing December 2014 Printed U.S.A.

HAZELRIDGE PRESS.

To Mom – For being there from babyhood until now. I know I didn't always make it easy.

CONTENTS

ACKNOWLEDGMENTS

I'm going to keep this short. *Owned by the Ocean* is a story that I absolutely love. Brant is a really important character to me and I really wanted to tell his and Catherine's story. This is it.

This story started out as my first winning NaNoWriMo (National Novel Writing Month) story. It then went on to be serialized on my blog for you, my readers. From there, I released it as a free eBook, and now, due to people continually asking when it will be in print—here it is.

I want to thank Elissa, Heather, and Andrew for giving me feedback and letting me bounce ideas off of you. I love how involved you all have become in the entire Ocean series and how you get just as excited over the characters as I do.

Thank you to my parents, your support is invaluable.

Thank you to the readers that responded with excitement, feedback and conversation. You all made writing and editing this book such a fun experience.

Thank you to my wonderful cover designer. You totally understood my vision and the end product is absolutely amazing.

Ellen MacDonald, you're my publicist, but you do so much more. Thank you for being here every step of the way, for giving me your expertise in publishing, print and design. I don't know where I'd be without you.

Lastly, I want to thank Kyle. Being married to a writer isn't always an easy thing but you always support and encourage me. Thank you.

CHAPTER ONE

England- 1660

Brant looked up from his scribbler at his teacher who was droning on about something to do with the politics behind the colonization of the new world... or was it the precarious peace with Spain? Either way, he didn't really care. Time was moving at a snail's pace. Every tick of the clock sounded like a hammer hitting an anvil. The boy two rows down was scratching his head; Brant was pretty sure he had lice. In front of him, another boy was drumming his fingers incessantly. Every noise and movement was grating and more in focus than Mr. Johnson's teaching.

Brant shut out everything around him and looked down at the open page of his scribbler. He was supposed to be writing notes, but instead the page was covered with carelessly doodled shapes or words that had nothing to do with what Mr. Johnson was teaching.

At sixteen, Brant Foxton had no interest in the politics, grammar, or math that filled each and every day at the school for young men he attended. All he wanted was to leave the masquerade called London society and sail. He had expressed this desire many times over to his father, *Sir* Calvin Foxton, but he would hear nothing of it.

Calvin Foxton had served his King faithfully for many years in both the army and then as a member of his council. He had been knighted when Brant was but five years old, a moment in history that he could remember being filled with excitement and honor for his father. Too bad it didn't take long for Brant to realize that he was treated more like a soldier than a son.

This past year, after many attempts at convincing his father to allow him to attend the royal naval academy, Brant had been sent to a prestigious boarding school in the heart of London, where he was to be polished and educated for service to the crown as the gentleman his family name required. There would be no sails, sword, or pistols in Brant's future. Instead it held paper work, money, and bowing and scraping before the King. That was the life of nobility in England and that was to be the life of Brant Foxton. That was his father's plan.

Brant stopped his doodling and looked around. Some of the boys were asleep, others intently taking notes and listening to the teacher. Most of the boys at this school were everything their parents expected them to be. The picture of young men of society, they walked and talked exactly as they were instructed, turned their noses up at those less fortunate than them, and flaunted money—that many didn't have but their name allowed them to pretend—like it was their job. They were raised to outwardly respect someone like Brant due to his family's status, but many whispered behind his back or snickered over their afternoon tea. Brant was an anomaly, someone who didn't care about prestige, money, and would very willingly throw it all away for a chance at a different future.

Brant was not an overly kind boy, nor humble. He hated his father and family name, he hated the school and the teachers, he hated the boys who hid behind masks their parents had forced on them, and most of all he hated that he was considered to be among them. He was better than this and he knew it. He was better than the acting and the back stabbing that he saw among the boys.

London was full of hypocrites. Brant may be blatantly cavalier and didn't give a damn, but the boys he went to school with participated in the same activities, just behind well-kept facades. No one but themselves and perhaps their closest friends knew about the things they did that their family would disapprove of. But they all did them. Brant had seen the older boys get drunk and steal things from the younger ones. He had seen, and been a victim of their bullying behind closed doors. But they all hid it from the outside world, from prying eyes. To the public, to the teachers, they were everything young gentlemen should be. Everyone but Brant Foxton.

The class was dismissed, and Brant left the room in a shuffle of feet and a murmur of voices. Politics had been the last class of the day and they now had the evening for free time until dinner was called. Brant went up to his room that he shared with two other boys and, lying on his bed, pulled out a military strategy book he had taken from the library. There was no military strategy class offered since the boys that went here didn't need to know about battle formations and military hierarchy. But, the library carried books on the subject, and Brant spent his free time educating himself on everything he would need to know to join the navy. He hoped that with the knowledge he gained from reading he would be able to make his way through the ranks quickly and become an officer in short order. Of course his father would not even consider forgiving him until he made captain, then perhaps he would think Brant was upholding the family name in an honorable fashion. But until he was prepared, he would remain in school and learn what he could, then take his leave and endure his father's disapproval.

Things had changed when Brant's mother passed away six years earlier. Calvin had become hard on his son, without his gentle wife to keep him in line. Brant's brother, James, who was now six, was mostly taken care of by a nurse and the maids. Calvin Foxton didn't have much time for his youngest son, not when he was reminded of his wife, who had died giving birth to him, every time he saw him. Brant guessed that his mother was the only person Calvin Foxton had ever been gentle with. He had been young when his mother passed, only ten, but from what he remembered she was a kind woman, and had truly loved her husband, which was not something he saw often among other couples.

It had been an arranged marriage, as many of them were, and Suzanne had been ten years Calvin's junior. However, they had fallen in love during their years together, and Brant was certain his father would have given Suzanne Foxton anything she wanted. If she gave him even a disapproving look when Calvin adopted his military background with his son he would immediately melt and become a loving and kind father.

That had disappeared when Suzanne passed away. Suddenly there was only military discipline and his father was detached from him in every way. No longer did Brant have loving parents but instead he had a commander and he was nothing more than a delinquent soldier. It had been a drastic change that had embittered Brant towards his father. He was convinced that if his mother was alive, he would have been allowed to join the Royal Navy. She had always wanted what was best for Brant and what would make him happy in the long run. Calvin would have nothing to do with that now. The military was not the place for his son, especially the sea. There was nothing glamorous about being an officer, captain, or commodore. They were respected if they served the king well and had some kind of military genius that brought them to his attention, but otherwise they were just another civil servant making low pay and risking their lives for honor that Brant shouldn't have to earn any longer. He was born with it.

Leo, one of his roommates walked in, took one look at Brant, and laughed.

"All you ever do is study those useless books. That won't help you at all with your marks here."

"I don't really care about my marks."

"You should. Your father is going to beat you if you fail."

Brant laughed. "He can try. I'm getting a bit old for him to slap around."

Leo was two years Brant's senior and had two years left in the school. He was looking to take over his father's business in Jamaica where he owned a sugar cane plantation.

Out of all the boys in school, Leo was probably the only one Brant considered a friend. In society Leo was what every young man should be, but in his circle of friends he was better known as a womanizer and a gambler. When his father sent him money, Leo made his way to a local brothel where he spent time with Claire, a pretty little blonde that had been used one too many times and had a sad look behind her eyes. He was kind to her though, and when he went out with the guys he would invite her along. Although her company was paid for, she was accepted among them as a friend. One couldn't help the circumstances life had dealt them.

When the money didn't come Leo would pull out his charm and woo a pretty second or third class girl that dreamed of a man like Leo coming along and marrying her, turning her into a real lady. It was never going to happen though. And every time, it was the same, hopeful laughter turning into disappointed tears. It bothered Brant that Leo could be so self-absorbed, yet he considered himself fortunate to be his friend.

Leo was kind enough to most of the boys, but he enjoyed putting some of the more pompous pricks in their place. When Brant had started out his year Leo had considered Brant just one of those; a pompous prick who curtailed off his daddy and thought himself better than everyone else. But, for the most part, Leo was humble and kind. He never considered other boys inferior, even if society deemed them so, and always treated everyone with respect. Even outside of society he seemed to ignore the boundaries and distinction and class and mingled without prejudice. That was what Brant liked about Leo. And for that, he overlooked his friend's less than upstanding behavior.

Leo and Brant were not so fortunate as to have the third boy who shared their room follow their life philosophies. Robert was a second year student, right between Brant and Leo. He was self-important and had delusions of grandeur. His family was on the verge of losing everything, and everyone knew it. Yet they held onto their expensive taste, threw just as many dinner parties as before, and turned up their noses at anyone they considered beneath them. They sent Robert to school on their good name and credit, but he strutted the halls as if his father was the King himself, and treated the younger boys with such disdain that you would have thought them his servants.

He never said a word to Brant or Leo after he discovered they had no interest in playing along. Instead, they took every opportunity to take him down a notch. A biting comment or a prank usually managed to put him in his place for a short time.

"Are you going home for Christmas?" asked Brant, looking up from his book.

Leo too had lay down on his bed and was studying his arithmetic. He looked over at Brant. "Of course. I believe my father is coming to get me next week. Are you?"

"I suppose. My father hasn't visited me except that one time I got in trouble for pouring ink down Robert's jacket."

Leo chuckled, presumably at the memory of Robert's face turning a plum shade of purple from anger and embarrassment. "He's a tough one, but I'm sure he only wants what's best for you."

Brant scoffed. "What's best for me? Perhaps, but he has a very narrow view of what's best."

Leo put down his book and sat up. "I like you, Brant, but I also think you're in serious need of an attitude adjustment. Your father has worked very hard to get where he is now and you don't appreciate what he has given you. He doesn't want his life for you. The navy is not easy and often ends in tragedy. Take the easy way. Your father worked hard so you would have the best things in life."

"It's not about status and courts and money to me. I don't want to be stuck in a life where everyone plays a role and wears a mask. I want adventure and freedom."

"Then you are naive. You think adventure is glamorous? If so, I think you will find yourself disappointed. This life isn't so bad. I have fun still."

"But your parents, anyone outside of your circle of friends, have no idea what you're truly like."

"That's not true. I still act like myself; I just choose to practice discretion in revealing some of my less than appropriate habits. Speaking of which, my father sent some money again. Would you like to go play some cards?"

Brant looked back at his book for a moment then sighed. "Why not? It's that or stay here reading."

Leo laughed. "That's the spirit. Come on let's dig into your trust fund a little and make use of some of your father's hard earned money."

* * *

Brant took another sip of whisky as he looked over his cards. He knew he had a decent hand but he wasn't sure he was willing to risk his money on it. He looked around from person to person. Leo grinned like a wild cat, but he always did. Whether he was winning or losing, it was easier for him to look happy than to keep a straight face. If Leo were to win, he would split the pot with Brant and they would stay out and have a good time. If anyone else were to win, both Brant and Leo would be out of luck and out of money. It would be back to school for them with their tails between their legs to await a week of boredom until they went home for Christmas.

Brant made his decision.

"I'm calling," he said, laying his cards down on the table face up.

The three men lay their cards down in a huff, most of them had nothing, one guy was close but fell just short of Brant's hand. Leo had yet to place his cards.

"Not bad, Brant, not bad. But you still have much to learn." Leo lay down a royal flush.

Sometimes Brant wondered if he cheated, because Leo had the best of luck at cards. It seemed he only lost when he had to.

Leo stood up and swept the money that had collected in the middle of the worn and dirty table into his hat. He and Brant walked over to another table where he began to count it.

"How much did you put in?"

"About ten pounds."

Leo counted out the money and handed it over to Brant. "Drinks are on me tonight, my friend. Consider it an early Christmas gift."

Brant laughed. "Thanks, but I didn't get you anything."

"Aw who cares, it is drinks. If you had been the lucky one tonight you'd be the one buying. Besides, if we really want to be a stickler about who's buying the drinks, it is the three guys we left sitting at the card table. Merry Christmas to us." Leo raised his glass and drained the last of the whisky.

Brant looked around the bar and took a long drink from his glass. Pulling a packet of cigarettes from his jacket, he offered one to Leo who took two, tucking one behind his ear and lighting the other.

"This is the life, Brant. All we need is a couple of girls on our arms and we'd be high class."

"We are high class, Leo."

"But we're boring high class. This is fun high class; drinking, smoking, and girls. We need us some girls.

"This life you're chasing after, my friend, has some of the qualities I'm looking for, I'll admit, but it is hard work and that is not something I enjoy. In another couple of years I'll be shipped off to Jamaica and I'll have all the drinks and smokes and girls I want without my father knowing and with money at my disposal."

"With an attitude like that, you'll run your father's plantation into the ground."

"Nah, you see I have business sense. I know when enough is enough."

Brant smiled. His friend was smart, but he did enjoy blowing his money. It worried him that he would be taking over his family's largest source of income.

"Leo, I think we should go back soon."

"Nonsense. I expect to have a good time tonight." Leo waved over a serving girl who brought him another whisky. "Hello, love, what's your name?"

She giggled, something Brant couldn't stand in the girls Leo chased. All so giggly and flirtatious. It was disgusting.

"Sarah."

"Well, Sarah, my friend Brant, could use some company. He doesn't think that being here is any fun. Do you think you can change his mind?"

She looked at Brant and giggled again. "Why this is the most fun pub in all of London. You can ask any one of the serving girls." She winked, put a drink in front of Brant and flounced away.

"Leo, that was sad."

"How so, my friend?"

"The girl is desperate for guys like us to take a liking to her. They all are. Those silly dresses they wear leave very little for the imagination, and she still thinks that a bit of attention from a guy like you or me will take her out of this hell hole and into our lives. It's sad. I'd rather pay a whore like Claire than play this game."

Leo's eyes flashed. "Don't call her a whore."

"That's what she is, Leo. She's a nice girl, and I wish just as much as you that she didn't have to sell herself, but that is the reality of things. Don't be angry with me that you're falling in love with a common prostitute."

Brant knew it was a low blow. He could see how his friend felt about the girl and he felt bad that Leo could never find the happiness he was searching for in Claire. They were of completely different classes and she was a scarlet letter. A harlot. If she was anyone, anyone at all other than what she was, Leo could risk bringing her into his world. But as a working girl, never.

Leo's face twisted in anger. "I'm not in love with her."

"No? I understand that you *can't* be in love with her, but don't lie to me; you're falling for her and you're too far gone to break it off. For goodness sake, Leo, you have to *pay* her to spend time with you!"

"That can change. She could leave the brothel."

"But do you honestly think she will? You called me naive earlier, but now who is acting naive? She has seen too much of the world. She knows no one like you or I are going to make good on taking her out of this life. As much as you might want to she knows you can't. Your family and society would never allow it. She's stuck with the hand she was dealt and the only thing you can do is continue to pay her to spend time with you."

"In two years I'm leaving for Jamaica. I can pay her passage and she can come along."

"Can she? Do you really think your father would allow you to run his plantation if you're keeping a mistress and having her gallivant around as a real lady?"

"He doesn't have to know."

"You're right, he doesn't, and I hope for yours and Claire's sakes that you can find a way to make it work. But it's unlikely. If you really want to make it work you may have to stoop down a level, leave your family name and fortune behind and make it on your own."

Leo got up and slammed his glass down. "When did I ask you for advice about my life, Brant? When did I ever ask for your input?"

"When did I ask for yours? You tell me I'm silly all the time but what are you?"

"I'll see you tomorrow. I'm not looking for advice from a sixteen year old that doesn't know anything about life. Not tonight. Not ever."

Leo threw a few coins on the table to cover the tab and left the bar. Brant knew he was off to see Claire and he would be back for breakfast tomorrow, so he didn't worry. His friend had to blow off some steam.

Once he finished his drink, he waved over the nearest girl and ordered another, leaning back in his seat and lighting another cigarette. Sarah, the serving girl came over, all smiles, drink in hand.

"Where's your friend?"

"He left."

"That's too bad. I don't suppose he'll be coming back?"

"No. Can I ask you something, Sarah?"

"Sure."

"Why do you do it? Why do you flounce around, smile and let people man-handle you? Will it get you anywhere?"

"It'll get me tips and put food on the table."

"I wish you would have more self-esteem, Sarah. You're worth more than this."

Sarah laughed bitterly. "Thank you, but I think I know what I'm worth. Not everyone can be born into wealth and privilege. Some of us have to paste on a smile, pull our necklines a little lower, and hope we come home with enough coin at the end of the day to get a family fed." She didn't stick around to hear Brant's response, and he was glad she didn't. He wasn't really sure what to say.

Getting up, he walked by where Sarah was standing near the bar, and as he passed, he slipped her a ten pound note.

CHAPTER TWO

Brant opened his eyes slightly as Leo stumbled into their room. Robert remained fast asleep as far as Brant could tell, but Leo was making a real racket, crashing into a dresser and then his bedpost as he felt his way blindly in the dark.

"You okay?" Brant whispered.

Leo fell onto his bed and sighed. "Do I look okay?"

"I'm sorry," and they both knew he wasn't talking about the bruises that Leo was sure to have in the morning.

"But you're right and I hate it."

Brant didn't reply so the two boys lay in silence. Brant waited until he heard Leo snoring, then got up and left the room. It was expressly against the rules to be out of the dorms after ten, but he left anyway. He needed time to think, time away from the supressing darkness and heavy breathing that filled his room.

Making his way to the study lounge, Brant stepped lightly in stocking feet, all the while listening for anyone that may be patrolling the halls. He didn't know what would happen if he was caught, but he didn't really want to provoke his father's anger, and there was no sense in being careless.

Sitting down in one of the large easy chairs beside the ever burning fireplace, in the cozy and quiet room, Brant sighed and rested his head in his hands. He hated seeing Leo unhappy because of his own stupidity, but he was no different. How many times had his friend urged him to embrace the life he'd been given? And yet he chose to be miserable as he strove for the one life he couldn't have.

He would be going home soon for Christmas and then he would be back here again to finish off the school year. He had four years of school to endure, and after only a few months he was beginning to wonder if he could do it. Already he had lost interest completely. He found himself fighting the urge to walk out of class and keep walking until he found himself a ship and was sailing beyond his father's grasp. He could do it, it wouldn't be very hard. All it took was a little resolve. But as much as Brant knew what he wanted, he couldn't bring himself to go against his father. In small ways, sure, breaking rules, drinking and smoking, playing pranks on the teachers; it all didn't matter. He hated to admit it, but the small acts of rebellion were to get his father's attention. It was his way of showing his father how incredibly unhappy he was with his life, and at the young age of sixteen he shouldn't be so unhappy. He shouldn't have to worry about whether or not he was going to be miserable all his life. He was too young to have that kind of weight. Was it too much to want the approval of his father for his life choices?

Pulling a cigarette out from the pack he always kept in his jacket pocket, Brant lit it and drew slowly back on the paper stick, letting the sweet, acrid smoke fill his mouth and filter down into his lungs, then curling and caressing his lips and nostrils as he exhaled. Instantly he felt his muscles relax.

"Brant Foxton?"

He quickly hid his cigarette and looked over to see who the voice belonged to. It was well past one in the morning and no one should have been walking around.

"Hello, Headmaster Mansfield."

"You do realize that it is well past curfew?"

"Yes sir," Brant replied, not a hint of apology in his voice, just simple admittance. He had learned quickly that the man was soft and would likely not do anything unless there was some serious harm in a boy's actions.

"It is also against the rules to smoke on school property."

"Would you like to join me?"

Headmaster Mansfield chuckled. "You know, I really would. I won't tell anyone if you won't."

"Deal." Brant handed the Headmaster a cigarette and his box of matches.

They sat in silence for quite some time, staring into the smouldering fire and smoking the forbidden cigarettes. Headmaster Mansfield attempted to make conversation a couple times, but Brant would only reply with one or two words and continue to smoke sullenly.

"You know, Brant,E I've heard a lot of things about you from the teachers. Not very much of it good. What is troubling you?"

"I just have no interest in what you have to teach."

"And what do you have interest in?"

Brant was a little taken aback. No one had ever shown interest in what *he* wanted. No one since his mother. "It doesn't matter; my life is already planned. I know you are trying to look after the well-being of your students, but don't waste your time on me. I'll be fine in life no matter what happens. I could smoke, drink, and gamble my youth away and I'd still have a fortune waiting for me. You don't have a bunch of well-behaved boys here, Headmaster. Just a lot of hypocrites."

Brant stood up and walked out, leaving Headmaster Mansfield alone with his thoughts. The man was soft… too soft. He didn't realize what was going on around him and he chose to turn a blind eye to much of the rule breaking. It was no wonder no one here had any respect for him.

Lying in bed Brant lit another cigarette… One of these days he would really have to kick the habit but right now it was just too good to let go. As the last of the ashes fell from the cigarette and onto the floor Brant stepped on the already cooling butt and then undressed. Sleep came quickly once he chose to close his eyes in the early hours of the morning. Tomorrow was another day, another day of broken dreams and disappointments.

* * *

Christmas came all too quickly, yet all too slow. Brant hated the idea going home and spending an entire month with his father, but the thought of leaving this place, if only temporarily, was undeniably attractive.

Sir Calvin Foxton's carriage pulled up at precisely twelve noon, just as he had told Brant it would. Brant sat on the steps with his bags and sullen attitude—he had been waiting in the cold for ten minutes. If there was anything that Calvin couldn't stand for it was tardiness. Especially when he was, out of the goodness of his heart, making the trip into London to pick up his son.

Brant had said goodbye to Leo that morning at breakfast. Their disagreement hadn't lasted longer than the one night, but Brant still worried about his friend. He seemed to be drinking more often, more than what Brant would consider recreational. He went to most of his classes slightly buzzed but the teachers gave no indication that they had noticed. How they missed it, Brant couldn't figure out. Leo reeked of booze and smoke. Drinking of any kind by the students was forbidden, but it seemed that the teachers preferred to turn a blind eye rather than deal with the issue.

Getting up from the step, Brant tossed his two small bags into the carriage and then stepped up, sitting on the bench opposite his father.

"Hello, son."

"Father."

"How are your studies going?"

"Fine. You get reports from Headmaster Mansfield, I'm sure, so you know."

"Yes, but I thought perhaps you would like to tell me how you're enjoying it."

"I'm not."

"I worked hard to be able to get you this kind of education."

"Officer training is a good education too."

"That is not a good life, Brant. It's beneath you. Try to remember who you are."

"I am a Foxton, son of Sir Calvin Foxton, former Commodore in the Royal Navy. You should be proud of me wanting to follow in your footsteps."

"It is a hard life and below you, no matter the recognition that comes with it. I came to bring you home for the holiday, Brant. I pay for you to have the best education. I will take no argument from you about what is best for your life. You're just a boy. That's all."

"So you'll just brush me off as if I'm no one? I'm not one of your sailors."

"Enough, Brant. I don't want to hear another word of this again. I have made my decision and you will accept that."

Brant knew better than to push his father any further. Calvin was not a soft man and when he reached the end of his patience the punishment doled out was more appropriate for an insubordinate sailor than a sixteen year old aristocrat.

The carriage ride was long; nearly two hours and it was spent in complete silence. Brant stared out the small window the entire way. He refused to look at his father, for fear of seeing the disappointed glare directed at his eldest son.

Calvin Foxton was gray and old before he should have been. His years as a sailor, officer, and commodore had aged him before his time, and the death of his young wife had only succeeded in making him bitter towards life. He was in his mid-fifties and yet had the appearance of someone much closer to seventy. His eyes were hard yet tired and full of sorrow. His strong jaw had lost all appearance of power, instead it looked hollow and unsuited to his weather worn and wrinkled face. His expensive clothes hung on a body that once boasted physical strength and prowess but had now been left soft and weak.

They arrived at the large Foxton estate still in complete silence, father and son refusing to speak to each other. Brant leapt out of the carriage as if to shove into his father's face his young and vital youth while his father slowly climbed out. The cold ride had stiffened his joints; joints that had been abused and worn down in their years of hard work and sleeping in damp cold. Brant had his two bags in hand and burst into the house, up the stairs and leapt onto the bed that he had missed for six long months.

He wondered how James had done, his six year old brother, alone in this large house with their father. There were, of course, maids and a nanny, but they could do little to stand in Calvin Foxton's way when his temper flared up. When thinking about his life at home, Brant came to the realization that his six months at school may be a blessing in disguise. He may not enjoy what he was being forced to learn but at least there was a distance between him and his father. At least at school he could escape. After all, security was lax and the Headmaster didn't seem to care as long as his students made a show of good behavior.

"Brant! Dinner will be ready in ten minutes. I expect you to be on time," his father shouted from down the hall. Apparently he didn't feel like having another confrontation with his son and had instead opted to keep his distance, something that was extremely out of character for the Commodore.

Brant chose not to respond and continued to lie on his bed. A whole month here in the hell hole of a house. There were too many ghosts walking these halls, of his mother in particular and of how their family used to function. He could remember the Christmas before his mother had died.

The three of them; Brant, his mother and father had spent the day together. They had saddled up their horses and gone for a long ride in the frosty air. The bluffs were beautiful at this time of year and Suzanne had always insisted in taking her daily ride to see them. Often Brant would accompany her but it was a rare occasion that Calvin would put his work down and join the wife he adored and his handsome young son.

Brant could remember laughing and racing his father all the way up the road and then back to join his mother. They had gone back to the house and hot tea had been waiting for them. They all sat around the fireplace in Calvin's study warming their frozen fingers, toes and faces while sipping at their hot tea and laughing about memories they had shared in the last year. Life had been good then, seven years ago. It had all changed so quickly and now it was nothing like it used to be. Christmas would be a short business affair with a few gifts for the two boys and then Calvin would be back to work while Brant and James would be expected to entertain themselves.

Brant got up and walked downstairs and into the dining hall. James and his father were already seated at the large table that hadn't been filled to capacity since before his mother had died.

Memories, they were all memories and they haunted Brant just as they haunted Calvin. James was spared knowing any life better than the one he spent with his detached father. He knew very little of his mother; she wasn't a comfortable topic of conversation and often left Calvin angry and on the rare occasion violent. Brant had learned long ago that it was better for everyone if Suzanne Foxton was never mentioned.

"How are you, James?" asked Brant upon sitting.

"Fine, thank you." Perfect manners from a perfect little six year old.

Dinner was spent in complete silence aside from the initial greeting Brant and James had exchanged. As soon as he was finished eating Calvin disappeared into his study where he would remain until long after both sons had retired for the evening. Brant and James were left alone together, Brant unsure of what to say to his young brother and James content to remain silent.

Brant had only been gone six months but already James had changed. He had become an empty shell. A man that followed orders rather than a happy and vibrant child. Gone was his playfulness, giggles and childlike awe. He was now subdued, silent, following perfect protocol like no human child should.

"James, are you okay?" How do you ask a six year old if he's unhappy? If he wants something different in life? He didn't understand being jaded. He couldn't comprehend not loving his father or accepting his wisdom. Brant knew this because he had struggled with those very feelings after his mother had died.

"What do you mean?"

"Do you like being alone here with father?"

"I'm not alone. Maggie and Josie and Markus and everyone else are here."

Brant smiled slightly. The servants; the only friends of a Foxton boy. "Did you miss me at all?"

James smiled. "There's no one to play with me when you're gone. Everyone is so quiet around papa and he gets angry when I get too loud so I learned to play by myself and be really quiet so I don't upset him."

Brant nodded. "That's very good, James. And then when you're my age you can go to school and learn stuff and have lots of boys your age to play with." The words seemed hollow, hypocritical, but he had to give something for James to look forward to.

"Is it lots of fun at school?"

Brant struggled with what to tell him. He was only six years old and he would likely grow up just the way the Commodore wanted, but he hated lying to the young boy. "It's so much fun. We play lots of games and learn lots of interesting stuff."

"I can't wait to go to school, Brant. Papa makes me learn boring stuff like my letters and he gets angry when I forget, but I try so hard."

"I'm sure you're doing a great job. Father just wants to make sure you do really well."

James smiled up at his big brother and leapt towards him, wrapping his small arms around Brant's much larger frame and squeezing him with what seemed like every ounce of strength in the six-year-old's body. The poor boy was starved for affection, and as much as he wanted his little brother to be happy, he couldn't help but feel that James was the reason his mother had died and had left him in this mess of a life. But James didn't deserve to be blamed and Brant knew that, it was just an impulse that occasionally reared its ugly head and Brant was forced to fight it off.

"I uh, am glad to see you again, James. I have to go for a walk," he said, gently peeling the boy off of him. He needed air.

"Can I come?" he asked eagerly, bouncing along at Brant's side as he walked towards to front door. His coat was hanging on the tree there and he grabbed it off while James jumped, trying to reach his.

Brant desperately wanted to go for a smoke but he couldn't very well do that in front of James. The Commodore smoked, most men did, but he would have been angry to know Brant had started. Smoking was a privilege reserved for men, not young boys. But he was disappointing his father at every turn, why not add smoking to the long list of transgressions?

"Sure, you can." Brant reached up and got his brother's coat for him. The small boy shrugged into it and struggled with the buttons.

"Here, let me help."

"I can do it."

"I'm not going to wait all night for you," teased Brant.

James got a stubborn look on his face, jutted out his tongue from between his teeth and slowly but surely got the buttons done up.

James jabbered the whole time they were walking while Brant responded with only the occasional "yes", "no" or "wow" to let his younger brother know he was still listening.

He pulled out a cigarette but James didn't seem to notice. Smoking one after another as his brother regaled him with tales. It wasn't until they turned back towards the house that Brant noticed James was shivering.

"Are you cold?"

"A little."

"You should have let me know. Come on let's get back and I'll see if Maggie can brew you some hot cocoa."

"Papa doesn't allow me to drink hot cocoa. He says it's bad for me."

Brant frowned. How could his father not allow James the simple pleasure of a hot treat? Some of his fondest winter memories were of drinking steaming cups of hot cocoa in front of a roaring fireplace. "That's nonsense. Hot cocoa makes young boys grow up extra handsome. I'm sure Maggie will make you some if I ask her."

The boys walked back into the house, Brant helping James hang his jacket on the much too tall coat tree and then leading him into the kitchen where Maggie was busy cleaning up for the end of the day.

"Hello, Maggie. Do you think James here could get a cup of hot cocoa? I'm afraid I kept him out in the cold a little too long."

"Ach! James me dear you take a seat there next to the fire and I'll have you a cup of steaming hot love brewed in not but a jiffy."

James smiled and sat down on the floor cross legged in front of the fire. Maggie had water boiling in minutes, having dropped everything she was doing to look after the young boy. As James sipped his drink Maggie sat down with Brant at a small table and handed him a cup of tea. "How be school, Brant?"

"It's everything you would expect, I suppose, and everything I don't want. It's my father's idea of a good education so I suppose I should be thankful."

"Your father ain't so bad. He's had it hard most of his life... those short years he had Suzanne were the only good ones."

"Shouldn't James and I be enough for him?"

"He don't know how to handle young boys. His whole experience with authority is his years in the navy. Your mother, bless her heart, was the one that told him how to handle you."

"How's James doing with him?"

"James don't know your father as anything other than the man he is today so he don't see anything wrong. Things are just the way things are. He's a good boy."

Brant nodded. "Thanks for the tea, Maggie. I think it's about time James got to bed though. I'm going to go find Josie and have her see to him."

"It sure is good to see you here again, Brant. I sure wish you'd smile like you used to. You're too young to have such a sad face."

Brant offered a smile, attempting a show at happiness for the old maid. She'd been around as long as Brant could remember and always had a smile or kind advice to offer when it was requested.

Brant left James in the kitchen as he went in search of Josie, James' nanny. She had been Brant's nanny as well, many years ago. She was a kind woman, and loved both boys dearly. Brant often wondered why she never left and found a nice man and settled down to have a family of her own but he suspected it would break her heart to leave James behind.

Brant lay in bed that night staring at the ceiling. He'd always thought that it was only a matter of time before his life held sails and endless water, but after today he wasn't sure he could leave. He felt responsible for James; could he leave him here alone and never look back? Brant knew that if he left he couldn't come back for years. James would be grown up by the time he saw him again. Was that something he could live with?

Brant fell asleep amid tumultuous thoughts of running away to the ocean or staying and living up to his father's dreams so that he could be an older brother to James. It wasn't a decision he could make in one day, or even in one lifetime. He had a month minus a day before school started. Brant knew that by the end of that time a decision had to be made. If he went back to school that would be it. If his father won this time around it would likely never change.

CHAPTER THREE

Christmas morning was no different than any other morning at home. The two boys and their father had breakfast together and then Calvin went into London to attend to business of some kind. Nothing stopped for the Commodore. Work, work, work every day and that was all that mattered.

James and Brant spent a lot of time together. Going for walks, rides, or working on James' schooling. Often, after their walks, they'd enjoy hot cocoa in the kitchen while Maggie prepared dinner. Brant had to admit that when his father wasn't around, he was really enjoying being home.

On December 27th, Leo rode up on his large standardbred stallion. Markus took the horse and led him away to the stables while Leo strode across the yard towards the large house. Brant, who had noticed his arrival, walked down the steps to meet his friend who was pulling off his gloves and blowing warm air into his cold hands. "Hello, Brant! How's your holiday going?"

"Oh, as good as can be expected. My father either locks himself in his study or is in London all day working, so at least I don't have to see him. But come inside, you must be freezing."

"Just a little." Leo followed Brant into the house where they sat down in chairs beside the crackling fire in the parlour and warmed their chilled fingers.

"And how are your holidays? Missing the city yet?"

"Immensely. It's so dull now that the Christmas festivities are over and New Year's hasn't arrived yet."

"There isn't a whole lot to do here either. James and I spend most of our days taking walks or reading."

"I think we both could use a little fun."

Brant chuckled, eager to hear what his friend had in mind.

"Can you get into your father's liquor cabinet?"

Brant's excitement immediately switched to wariness; he couldn't forget the mess Leo was in just before holidays and alcohol seemed like the last thing he needed. But, it was dull and Leo always knew how to have a good time. "I can. One moment."

Brant left the room for a few minutes and was back with two tumblers and a bottle of whisky. He poured the amber liquid and handed a glass to Leo.

"I don't know if I'll be coming back to school," he stated, matter-of-factly, as he placed the bottle on the table between them.

Leo sputtered, choking a bit on his drink and looked and Brant, shocked. "What do you mean? Did something happen?"

"No, nothing happened. I've just realized if I'm going to leave I have to do it now." Brant surprised himself a little with the conviction of his words. He'd thought of little else these past couple of weeks, but he hadn't come to a decision. Saying it out loud to Leo had been is way of testing the waters, to see how he really felt and he realized that his mind really was made up. He would leave everything behind for the chance at the life he wanted.

"Brant, this is insanity! You have everything you could ever need for the rest of your life."

"You wish you had the freedom to be with Claire and to change her life for the better, don't you? Well, I wish I had the freedom to do what I've always wanted to. When I was a boy my mother used to take me down to the wharf to watch the ships sail away. I used to dream of what adventures those vessels would embark on and I wanted that for myself—I still want that."

"It's hard work, the life of a sailor. Don't think it is all swashbuckling stories."

"I know, but that doesn't change how I feel about the sea. I need to go out and experience it."

Leo sighed and his shoulders slumped a little in defeat. "What can I do to help?"

"Nothing for me. Just... be around for James after I leave. Make sure he's doing okay."

"Of course. When are you going to leave?"

"The next few days. I'll ride to the docks and hopefully leave before my father can track me down. After I'm gone he won't bother with me. I'll be dead to him."

"Will you talk to James before you leave?"

"No. He might tell someone. Could you explain things to him after I'm gone?"

"If that's what you want."

"You're a good friend, Leo. Thank you."

"Don't mention it, please. Helping you will dirty my pristine reputation." Leo laughed, but Brant could see there was sadness in his eyes, a sense of loss.

Brant only shook his head and finished the last of his drink. "Your reputation was tarnished about when you started cavorting with me."

"True. Perhaps your leaving is a good thing. It might save me."

Brant smiled. Nothing kept his friend down for long, at least not outwardly. He was going to miss Leo. He never judged Brant for his decisions or choices, even if they were contrary to what he might believe or enjoy. Leaving this life, school, home, his father behind would be easy. Leaving behind Leo and James... that would be nearly impossible.

* * *

Brant spent the next few days with James. He played games with the young boy like hide and seek and tag. Every day with Brant he seemed to open up a little more, revert to his natural childlike tendencies. He no longer had to act the part of an adult like he did around his father. For a few days James got to be a six year old and it made Brant feel better that he was able to give his brother that much before he left.

On the day he planned on leaving, Brant took James out horseback riding. They spent dinner in silence though as their father joined them. After that James was taken to bed and Brant was left to his own devices. He walked throughout the entire house, in and out of rooms that he would likely never see again. When he was sure his father had gone to bed Brant went to his own room and packed a bag with a few necessities and then walked out the front door and to the stables. He quickly saddled one of his father's horses and mounted; riding down the lane he stopped the horse and looked back. The house was dark and not a movement was made. Brant smiled, stroked his horse and turned it back towards town. Tonight was the start of the rest of his life. He had made his choice and now it was time to live with it. Out of the corner of his eye Brant noticed the curtain in his father's study move slightly. Brant was leaving his father's life for good. That was the second loss in the Foxton household in six years. Would there be more?

* * *

Brant tied his father's horse on a hitching post and left him. Someone would claim him come morning, whether it was his father or someone else. It didn't really matter to him anyway.

Walking down the docks it was quiet. It was not the right time of day to be looking to join a crew, but he knew the taverns along the way would house a few crews who might know of a ship he could join.

Walking into one particularly loud one he found himself a seat and took out a smoke. It didn't take long for an older man to approach him.

"And what might a fine young man like you be doing in a place like this?"

"Looking for a billet."

"I see. And why might that be? From yer clothes I'd say you ain't in need of money."

"I prefer to keep my past to myself. Do you know of any place for me?"

"Aye I might. I take it you have no experience on a ship?"

"None, but I'm a fast learner and a hard worker."

"Our cabin boy just left us, perhaps I can convince the Cap'n to take ya on. What be yer name?"

"Brant Foxton."

"Aye, Brant. I'm Karl. You just sit tight 'ere for a few minutes and I'll let'ya know."

Karl was only gone a few minutes before he came back with another man.

"Brant, I'm Captain LaFleur of the *BlackFox*. Karl tells me you are in search of a ship." He spoke with a heavy French accent but he seemed friendly enough.

"Yes sir. Anything you got I'll do. I'm just looking to make a life on my own."

"We sail tomorrow. Will you be ready?"

"I'm ready to leave now."

"Good. Report for duty at first light. We'll put you to work. I'll have Karl waiting for you on dock twelve with a rowboat. He leaves at six... Don't be late."

"Yes sir. I'll be there, sir."

* * *

Brant had nowhere to sleep, and no money to pay for a room, so he left the tavern and made his way to dock twelve. There, he found himself a corner beside a building that emanated some heat to chase away the winter cold, and curled up as tightly as he could, hoping sleep would find him. It wasn't comfortable by any means, but at least it was quiet. Dock twelve was far away from most of the traffic and abandoned aside from the rats that slunk around barrels and crates looking for food.

Brant huddled closer to the thin walls of the building, wishing the slight warmth would chase away the chill that was creeping into his limbs. It took hours, but eventually the cold and exhaustion allowed him to drift off.

Brant probably managed to get two or three hours of sleep before a hubbub of working men roused him. His joints were stiff from the cold but he slowly sat up and stretched, working the blood down into his extremities as they tingled painfully to life. When he stood up he spotted Karl almost immediately, barking orders at a few men who seemed to be loading a row boat with supplies.

Karl looked up as Brant approached and gave a little wave.

"What ya doing 'ere already, boy?"

"Figured it's better to show up early than late."

Karl studied the boy carefully, his eyebrows furrowing, as if deep in thought, then, once he'd come to a conclusion, his face broke into one of the warmest smiles Brant had ever seen, crooked and stained teeth adding a comedic sense to the picture. "Well, I dare say we ain't gonna stop ya from working. You can help Joseph over there. He'll tell ya what to do."

Brant nodded and walked towards the middle aged man who was helping steady the load in the row boat.

"Hello, Joseph?"

"Aye. What do ya want?"

"Karl sent me to help you."

"Well don't just stand there like a nancy, get in 'ere and help me stabilize this here stuff."

Brant jumped in, causing the row boat to rock precariously. Joseph only threw his hands up in disgust. "You don't know what yer doing, do ya, boy?"

"Not really," he admitted, heat rising in his face. "But I'll learn fast. I've done a lot of reading and—"

"All the readin' and learnin' ain't gonna help ya out here. You gotta work hard and learn hard and you'll either die tryin' or become a man. Can ya handle that, boy?"

"Sure can. I'm not afraid of hard work. The name is Brant, by the way."

Joseph chuckled. "Yer lucky I like you, Brant, cause I got a mind ta throw ya overboard. Now, enough jabberin'."

Joseph pushed Brant hard but in an hour the row boat, which Brant learned was actually called a long boat, was full to the brim with supplies. The men working on the dock climbed in, positioning themselves amongst the crates and barrels, and rowed the large boat towards their ship; the *BlackFox,* where they tied her up and worked at hoisting box by box up onto the ship and into the hold. It was slow, gruelling work. Brant had rope burns and slivers in his hands and he was pretty sure he had blisters on top of blisters, but he never once stopped. He had to prove himself to these men or he would be sent back to his father sooner than an angry wasp will sting.

With the last box loaded Brant went to follow Joseph as Karl began to shout orders about hauling anchor and this person to the helm but Captain LaFleur grabbed his shoulder.

"That's enough, son. You're more likely to get in the way now than help. You'll learn in time. Come with me, I'll show you where we're headed."

Brant followed the captain to his cabin where he pulled out a large map and spread it over his desk, pinning down the corners with various heavy objects.

"We are heading into the Caribbean, here." He pointed to an area on the map. "We will be trading for sugars and such to bring back to France and England, officially."

Brant studied the map. "And what do we do unofficially?"

"Well, I would say pirate but that is such an awful word. I prefer to think that we relieve certain enemy ships of their goods to provide ourselves with profit."

"I see."

"Is there a problem, Mr. Foxton?"

Brant's throat tightened. He hadn't been looking for piracy, or privateering. He'd wanted a good, upstanding ship to get him experience so he could join the Royal Navy. But now he was among dangerous men, and his future hung on how he chose to answer. "No problem here, Sir."

"Good man. Don't worry, I'll keep you out of the foray until you're ready. I'll train you with the blade myself and the master gunner can show you the cannons and guns. Have you had any formal training?"

"No sir."

"That's a shame."

"You'll have a blank slate to work with. Should make things easier."

"Perhaps. I do believe we are underway now; Karl has stopped his hollering. Shall we take a spin around deck?"

Brant nodded and followed Captain LaFleur once again. The captain showed him all the gun ports, hiding places, what different rigs did and what not. It was overwhelming. They stopped at the starboard side of the ship and looked out to the ocean. England was slowly disappearing along the horizon.

"Forgive me for saying, sir, but you and your crew don't strike me as pirates."

Captain LaFleur laughed. "Of course not. We aren't the criminal sort. We're employed by the King, although if we get caught by the Spaniards we can never admit to that. We are of the respectable sort or pirate, if those exist; Privateers, my young friend."

"Privateering doesn't make it right. You're still killing people for greed." Brant felt bold, confident to speak his mind due to the kindness of his captain.

"We are waging a private war, my boy, no better or worse than a public one. I don't pretend to think that what I do is moral, but someone has to do it and I'm good at it. Believe me, I'll be asking for a priest to take my confession when I'm on my death bed."

Brant smiled. "What should I be doing?" he asked, changing the subject.

"For now, wander and stay out of the way. Meet the men and try not to make any enemies; these are cramped quarters we share. Karl will let you know if there are things to be done, but you worked hard this morning and I'm pleased with you. You might do okay out here."

CHAPTER FOUR

The loud boom of cannon fire shook the ship and the planking beneath Brant's feet as he ran down the cramped hall below deck with a heavy iron ball clutched between his hands.

"Hurry up there, Foxton!" shouted Joseph, who was waiting impatiently for the cannon ball to reload the huge gun that had already been wheeled back from its port. "Yer gonna need to bring more than one at a time," he growled as he snatched the ball from Brant's hands and rolled it down the nose of the cannon.

Brant only nodded and ran back down the hall to where the ammunition was kept. Struggling to lift two balls into his arms, he hurried back down the ship, dodging men and guns in the flurry of activity that was occurring below deck.

The constant booming of firing cannons left Brant's ears ringing and his mind disorientated. It took all he had just to remain standing upright as cannons leapt backwards in plumes of smoke and the deck rolled beneath his feet.

He couldn't hear the clashing of swords, the screams of pain and death, the metallic smell of blood, or the yells of victory that he was sure were taking place somewhere above, on this ship or the one they had locked in a dance to the death. No, Brant could only hear the ringing and booming that came with cannon fire. He could only smell the acrid smoke of gunpowder and singed skin of over-eager sailors. He only felt the burning protest of his arms as his muscles screamed at him for a moment's rest, a moment's relief from the heavy load they'd been carrying for what seemed like hours.

And then, almost as quickly as it had all begun, it grew silent.

But it was far from over. As he exited the dark hold into the bright sunlight, the smell of death bombarded him. Despite the salty sea air, there was no escaping the sickly sweet smell that seemed to cover the ship in a haze of despair. Brant felt his stomach protest and ran to the rail, heaving his breakfast over the side and gasping for breath.

A rough hand rested gently on his shoulder. "You okay, son?"

Brant turned to face Karl and nodded slowly, wiping at his mouth with his dirty sleeve. "I will be."

"First time is always the hardest. You'll get used to it."

He shuddered. "I'm not sure I want to—" he trailed off and looked back out to the open water, the sight of the blood stained deck threatening to have him heaving over the side again.

"This is a hard life, boy. Death and pain are an unfortunate reality. Is that somethin' you can handle?"

Could he? He breathed in fresh sea air. With each exhale he felt calmer. When he'd first left London he'd wondered if he'd live to regret this decision, but up until this point he'd loved it. Loved swabbing the decks and helping the cook prepare dinner. He loved washing laundry and revelled in the blisters that covered his hands from ropes and mops and swords. It was exciting to practice sparring with Captain LeFleur and Karl, feeling the power of a pistol firing, or loading a cannon. There was something about going to bed each night exhausted and waking up each morning eager to see what the day held in store that had Brant feeling more alive than he ever had.

But could he learn to live with death? To become efficient at taking lives without a second thought, all in the name of blood stained gold?

Brant looked up at Karl's smiling face, his kind eyes showing concern for the boy, and slowly nodded. "In time."

***

Brant had been sailing with the crew of the *BlackFox* for nearly three months when they docked in Port Royale, Jamaica. Here, they paid a portion of what they had taken to the governor, who would report it as profits to the king; keeping their business legitimate and their necks comfortably noose free.

Port Royale was everything Brant had dreamed it would be; exotic, noisy, busy, and in no way industrialized like London. It was beautiful, with palm trees swaying in the breeze and white sand making up beaches along the island's edge. The word that came to mind when he walked through the streets was something akin to paradise.

Brant sat next to Corbin, the sailing master aboard the *BlackFox,* in a dingy bar. He glanced down at his cards, a two of clubs, five of spades, a nine of hearts, and two queens. That, paired with the cards on the table, he had nothing. He took a long drag of his cigarette, then threw his cards on the table. "I fold."

He glanced over at Corbin, who tapped his finger twice against the back of his hand of cards. He had a good hand. This was the third round Brant had folded and his pockets were beginning to grow light.

They made a few more rounds of bets and then a smug looking young man, who looked much too well-dressed to be found in an establishment such as this, called.

One by one the men lay down their cards, Corbin included. The smug man had a run, and with a smirk he swept the coins down the table towards himself, pocketing the small pot. It was nothing extravagant, but it was a good portion of many of the men's wages sitting around the table. Wages that were nothing more than pocket change and a good time for the man who had won. Brant was beginning to understand why people hated it when he and Leo had played. Because rich boys and men did not belong at the same table as the desperate and poor. Here, it was more than just a game; it was an escape, it was hope that they'd be able to bring home a few pounds more for their wife and children. When you lost, the men understood what that meant. People like Leo, like this young man, like the person he used to be, did not.

Brant pushed back his chair and walked out of the pub in disgust. It wasn't so much that he'd lost the money. It didn't matter for him. He had no one to send wages home to. It was that he used to be that man. He used to be the one taking hard earned money from those less fortunate, and it made him sick.

Corbin didn't follow him out, and he assumed his friend had stayed to either play more cards, or join a couple other crew members who had deposited themselves at a table and were filling themselves with drink.

It was growing dark as Brant made his way down the docks back towards the *BlackFox*. The men had all been given a couple days leave while they recuperated from the three months in cramped quarters.

He walked up the gangplank aboard the ship. It was mostly deserted. A single lantern hung near the mast, illuminating a small portion of the deck, and Karl who was sitting beneath it. Smoke curled out from the man's pipe, and drifted out to the open water. Brant could see a glow coming from the captain's cabin, where he would likely burn the midnight oil going over books and routes in preparation for their departure.

Taking a seat next to Karl, Brant reached into his pocket and pulled out a cigarette. He'd gone without for most of the three months voyage and the first thing he'd done upon docking was buy more.

"Had enough of the shore?" asked Karl after a long stretch of silence.

Brant was slow to respond as he listened to the waves slapping against the hull of the ship, and the various noises from the town drifting towards them. "A little too much reality for me."

Karl chuckled and took another drag on his pipe. The smoke was sweet and reminded Brant a bit of the woods back home.

They sat for a few hours, Karl smoking his pipe and telling Brant stories of his younger years. It was nice to sit on a quiet deck with the man that had taken Brant under his wing.

"You shouldn't smoke those," said Karl, during a break between stories.

Brant had just lit another cigarette, and he looked down at it. "You're right, I haven't had any since my pack ran out over two months ago."

"It's the act. Relaxes you."

Brant smiled and nodded. "Old habit from an unhappy time of life."

"Yer too young to carry that weight."

"I'm not the first son to disappoint his father, to lose his mother too young. We do what we can with the cards we're dealt."

Karl chuckled and stood up slowly, stretching his stiff limbs. "Aye, we do. And men like you rise to the occasion. Mark my words, Brant, you'll have a life to be proud of yet."

Those were Karl's parting words of the evening. He strode away to his cabin and left Brant sitting alone, contemplating words spoken by a man who had become more of a father to him than Calvin Foxton ever was.

Two days later, as they sailed away from Port Royale, Brant took a few minutes to watch the retreating shoreline. His father owned a sugar plantation somewhere on the island, but he'd never seen it, never left the confines of England until now. Had his father been there, on his yearly trip to oversee it? Could they have been walking the same streets these past few days and not run into each other? He shook his head, dislodging the thoughts. The chances of his father being there were slim, at best. And even if he had been, and even if they'd seen each other, he knew there would be no acknowledgement. He'd made the choice to leave; he was dead in his father's eyes now.

* * *

Months went by, days of hard work melding into each other. It seemed like yesterday that Brant had sailed away from Port Royale. The only sign of passing time was his continued improvement at sparring and the growing pile of wooden barrels and chests in the hold.

Brant had become more accustomed to raids; the noises and smells no longer bothering him. And in the months since leaving Port Royale, he had been promoted from cabin boy to sailor, allowing him to collect a larger portion of pay and no longer being required to swab the deck or clean the latrine. But it wasn't enough, not yet. He wanted to be sailing master.

Many times he'd watched Corbin plot out a course using his tools and the stars. He'd adjust the rudder by centimeters, to keep them from sailing kilometers off course. He wrestled the ship against winds and won. It was the perfect mixture of science and strength, and it fascinated Brant.

It was good work, respectable. Maybe not enough to write home to his father about, but it was a start, and it was a goal he could work towards.

Brant's seventeenth birthday came, no different than any other day. He wouldn't have even realized if he hadn't been going over some of the navigation tools with Corbin and he had mentioned the date.

"It's my birthday," he said, working with the astrolabe.

"Yer birthday? How many years?"

Brant shrugged, not wanting to make a big deal out of it. "Seventeen."

"That be a year deserving of a drink."

Corbin disappeared down to the hold for a few minutes, leaving Brant alone on deck, feeling a little silly that his friend was even acknowledging a day that seemed so trivial and childish.

Corbin returned with a dusty bottle of rum, and took a swig before handing it over to Brant. They drank together as Corbin showed Brant the different uses for the tools he had laid out on the deck in front of them.

"You done real good for yerself," he told Brant as he packed away his leather pouch of instruments. "Cap'n is pleased with yer work and you be well on yer way to being the best swordsman we have on board."

"And yet Captain LaFleur will not let me fight."

"Cap'n won't be appreciatin' me saying this, but he's a softy. He ain't eager to send anyone into the fray until they've proven they can hold their own. Soon you'll be up there. You can best nearly anyone on the ship, just gotta let the Cap'n know yer ready."

Brant nodded and took another swig of rum. "Are you looking forward to summer leave?" he asked, changing the subject.

"Aye, it's been too long since I seen my wife. You have family waitin' for you?"

Brant's mind went briefly to James, but he shook his head. "It's just me."

"Yer welcome to stay with me and the wife. The house ain't much, but it's a roof over yer head."

* * *

Two months of leave went by uneventfully, and Brant found himself happier than ever to be back on the *BlackFox* and sailing again. He had spent the summer storm months with Corbin and his wife, Anna, helping them with various repairs Anna needed done before they left. In the evenings Corbin taught him the more intricate science of navigation; how to map and read the stars and use the more delicate instruments in his arsenal.

Every day he found time to spar with Corbin, more to keep himself in shape and on edge than to really challenge himself. Corbin was by no means an expert swordsman.

Their days were full, but when the day came to load up and sail out, Brant was eager to be at sea again; eager to feel the freedom and adventure and the satisfying ache in his bones after a day of hard work. This season held a lot of promise. He had one season under his belt, and he had done well. But now, with the second season upon him, his goals were that much closer, he could almost grasp them.

He knew that there would be no more manning cannons during a raid. He was good with the cutlass; he'd proven himself time and again to LeFleur in daily lessons. He'd bested nearly every man on the crew at one time or another, including Karl. He was ready, and he knew it. LeFleur needed good sword hands and he couldn't afford to squander the skills he had at his disposal; skills that Brant had worked hard to hone, not only with the blade, but working hard to learn the science of navigation from Corbin, something that was above and beyond his duties as a sailor. The *BlackFox* had no sailing mate to work under Corbin. That job was there, waiting for LeFleur to see Brant's potential and promote him.

He strolled the decks with Corbin, pulling the second watch of the night.

"This is my last season," said Corbin, out of nowhere.

Brant stopped his forward progression and looked at his friend. "What do you mean?"

"Anna, she be pregnant. It's time I went home and was a husband to her."

"Congratulations," and he meant it. He felt a twinge of pride for his friend, who was embarking on a new stage in his life.

"Cap'n is gonna need a new sailing master. I talked to him today, he is gonna promote you to sailing mate so you be ready to take over when I leave."

"When?"

"Soon."

"Thank you, Corbin."

They continued their watch, talking about what Corbin would do in the future as he settled into a quieter life as a father and husband. But Brant's mind was stuck on the fact that he was going to get what he was working towards, sooner than he expected.

He was busy mending a sail when Joseph approached him a few days later.

"The Cap'n wants to see you."

Brant jumped up. He'd been waiting for this since Corbin had broken the news, and was beginning to worry that perhaps Captain LeFleur had changed his mind, that there was someone older, more experienced and better suited to the position.

"You wanted to see me, Sir?" he asked, walking into the captain's cabin.

"Yes, Mr. Foxton. I've heard a great deal of good things about you from Corbin, and he seems to think you are in need of a rank change… perhaps sailing mate?"

Brant smiled broadly. "I'd really like that, Sir."

"He tells me that you've been learning the skills needed on your own time. I'm impressed."

"Thank you, Sir."

"Which brings me to another matter: I don't believe your skills are best utilized on the cannon deck during raids."

Brant's heart quickened. This was it. Only a few weeks at sea and he was getting everything he'd hoped for.

"You'll be on the boarding party next raid. I think you've proven yourself more than ready."

"Thank you, Sir. I won't disappoint you."

LeFleur nodded and looked back down at the papers spread over his desk. "Now, I believe you have work to do."

* * *

Brant's opportunity to join in a raid came quickly. The *BlackFox* followed heavily used trading routes, and were never long between attacks. When the first cannon shot fired and the deck shook beneath his feet he felt the first inkling of apprehension. Each cannon blast only succeeded in escalating his fear. He glanced around nervously at the waiting men, who seemed eager to spill blood. A buzz of adrenaline filled the deck and yet he felt himself shaking in fear. It was one thing to spar, never drawing blood; it was completely different to take over a ship and kill men for nothing more than gold and stores, all in the name of weakening an enemy of the crown.

When the order came to board, Brant lunged forward with the rest of the men, screaming and yelling their bloody war cries, but not feeling the hu-rah that the other men seemed to possess.

There was no chance to collect one's thoughts when he landed on the deck of the other ship. Immediately someone charged at him with a sword ready to cut him open. Brant parried and thrust skillfully, protecting his life and fighting to take another's. This was different from sparring. There was no cool calculation of moves and steps. Out here men fought with desperation, and screams of death overpowered the music of clashing steal.

There was no one-on-one or rules of engagement. An attack could come from any angle, from any number of men. Bullets whizzed by, and you could only pray that one didn't find its mark in you.

Brant felt a sharp pain in his side and he looked down; a growing red stain covering his dirty white shirt.

"Don't!" Corbin's blade jumped into view and blocked a thrust. "Brush it off or yer dead!"

It was enough to shake Brant out of the stupor the sight of his blood had put him in, and his sword arm was immediately back at work, but his vision spun a little. It had just become a little more real; if Corbin hadn't been right there he would have been run through, because he stopped for a split second. That was all it took; a second.

For Brant the fight seemed to take forever but in reality it went quickly. The crew surrendered and LaFleur had their hold cleaned out of anything valuable, and then the ship was left to flounder in its ruined state. Corbin took Brant directly to the surgeon to have his stab wound looked after, but he kept assuring Brant that it was nothing to be worried about.

After getting his wound cleaned and stitched, he joined the rest of the crew to stow things away below deck. His side ached, reminding him of how close he'd come to death, but he was proud of himself. Death hadn't left him weak-kneed or nauseous. He had held his own, and in time he would get better.

He'd told Karl after the first raid that he'd learn to live with it, that he'd be okay with death, and he was. He never lost his composure again after that first raid. But after seeing the life leave a man's eyes, he understood what Captain LeFleur had meant when he said ghosts haunted him. Brant wanted to hurt for the men that he had killed this afternoon and never forget the look in their eyes as their souls left their bodies.

As he celebrated their victory that night with the crew, he took a swig of rum and passed the bottle on, listening to stories of close calls and staring death in the face. Brant smiled and laughed, he showed off his wound and the men congratulated him on his first stabbing, a rite of passage it seemed. But underneath all the bravado and laughter, he was hurting, hurting for the men that he had taken from loving mothers and waiting wives. He vowed to remember each life he took, so that when judgement day came and he had to atone for the sins he'd committed, he'd know the face of each and every man that testified against him, and he'd know that he deserved to suffer for eternity.

CHAPTER FIVE

Three Years Later- 1663

Brant's eighteenth birthday came and went, then his nineteenth. Three years he'd served aboard the *BlackFox,* spilling more blood than he cared to measure, developing calluses on top of calluses, spending countless hours working harder than he ever thought was possible; and he loved every minute of it.

Corbin had taken his leave, true to his word, after their second season working together, and was working as a cartographer in Port Royale. He hoped to take his wife and young son to the new world and map out the large and wild land, but the last Brant had heard he had no real plans to leave yet. Maybe it was all talk.

Brant had continued to learn the skills required of a sailing mate from Captain LeFleur after Corbin had left, but he had been told that for this voyage he was taking over as sailing master. No more sailing mate. Now he answered to no one, served no one but Captain LeFleur. And he would happily serve the man that had offered him so much until he could get a ship and a crew of his own. When that day came, he would sail to England and face his father with pride. He wondered from time to time how James was doing, but over three years had passed since he had seen him. He assumed James was doing well... he would be ten now, and probably still acting like the perfect disciplined boy he'd been when Brant left. Shaking the thoughts of his past, of a family he left behind, out of his head, Brant joined Captain LaFleur in his cabin to look over their intended course.

He had attended countless numbers of these meetings when he had been learning under Corbin and then LaFleur, but now it was his turn to take charge. He knew what to do. In the last year he had pretty much been doing everything himself with LaFleur only watching over his shoulder and putting in suggestions when needed. He was confident in his knowledge and in his skills, and he knew that he wouldn't fail; nevertheless it was a daunting thing to be called before the captain to do the job he had been trained in completely on his own for the first time.

Brant looked over the map that LaFleur was showing him and pointed at a location. "Here is where we're at. We're traveling at about fifteen knots right now. You want to get to Tortuga, best way would be along here," Brant explained as he traced a route along the worn paper.

"But?" asked LeFleur.

"Won't be many ships along this route."

LeFleur nodded. "I want to take the most direct route to Tortuga so we can empty the hold. We're sitting low in the water and it's slowing us down too much. Also, we can't keep having Harold do repairs on the ocean like this. We've taken too much damage in the last few raids."

"We should try to avoid storms as much as possible. It's getting late in the season. Could be some big ones starting to brew." Brant had been watching the sky earlier. He didn't like the look of the clouds that seemed to be chasing them down faster than they could sail, and he wasn't sure that the *BlackFox* was in any shape to weather a big gale. LeFleur had pushed them hard this season, barely letting them make port, having Harold do repairs on the run as much as possible. The last raid they had to run from with their tail between their legs, their beautiful ship barely limping away.

"It is, but we have to go a bit longer. We'll dock at Tortuga and spend the summer months there."

"If you don't mind me asking, Sir, why Tortuga? We just left Port Royale."

"Port Royale is taking in heavy trade and I don't want to trade, I want gold. Tortuga is a good place for that."

"Gold that is not taxable to the King?"

"If we play our cards right."

Brant pressed his lips together, holding back the words that were brewing inside. LeFleur was taking risks; pushing both the men and his ship harder than ever; going later into the season than was advisable; and now trying to cheat the king of gold that was, according to the letter of Marque, rightfully his.

LeFleur was getting up in age. Was he trying to cash in for retirement? Whatever it was, something wasn't adding up.

Brant took his leave and went to set the ship on the course they discussed. It was a time consuming job, but he had a good crew that could adjust the sails quickly and efficiently for their purposes. Of all the crews Brant could have been serving with, without this group of men—as rough as they were—he wouldn't be where he was today.

* * *

The summer storm months were usually dull, but this year was particularly so. Normally the crew settled in Port Royale, and Brant would spend the months with Corbin and Anna. There, he had some semblance of a family. Tortuga, though, was nothing but women, drinking and cards, which sounded good in theory. The women were boring and frivolous, only spending time with the men for money, and the entertainment was often drinking and bar brawls—which was good for a few laughs until it landed you in lock up for a night.

Brant spent most of his time with the men in his crew, throwing away all their money on rum and cigarettes. Many of the men had some girl on their arm that they had paid for, but Brant mostly ignored them. He had no interest in a girl that was merely giving away her body and not her heart.

Women weren't in his future. He didn't live a life he could bring one into, and he'd come to terms with that about when Corbin gave up his position to look after his family. He was lonely, but he refused to lower his standards for a one night lie. He'd seen what that did to Leo, and he didn't want that.

Brant finished off his glass of rum and noisily dropped it onto the wooden table. He was sick of hearing the girls in this bar laugh and flirt, pushing themselves on inebriated men. Was this how girls had been around Leo? He could remember thinking they were pathetic, but they were looking for a life change. These girls were just looking to make a pound.

Brant played with the idea of taking one up to his room… It would be so easy, just one night of reckless abandon that he could forget about the next day. Sooner or later a girl would come up to him if he watched them long enough. There was one girl who looked younger than the rest, wearing a dress that barely covered her chest. She was laughing at something another girl was saying to her. She was blushing… Either she was incredibly good at what she did, or she was new enough to still have a little bit of innocence about her. She looked over and caught Brant's eye. It was just a second, but it was enough. She sauntered over.

"You've been watchin' me."

"You aren't like the other girls. What's your story?"

"It's long… I got the time to tell it, if you got the money."

Brant smiled. "I got money. Sit, let me buy you a drink."

She sat and Brant waved over a serving girl and ordered two rums.

"I'm Brant."

"Clarice."

"You're too young to be working this job, Clarice. Too pretty."

"Mayhaps, but it is good money and I need it. My father died a little while back, he was a sailor, and me mom and baby brother are left with nothing. We don't have two shillings to rub together, so I do this. It's the one thing us women can do to make a decent penny, and I ain't gonna let my momma and baby brother go out on the street."

"Is that your real story, or is that the one your mistress told you to tell?"

"You think men around here give a lick about women being put out of their own homes? That's the truth. For every other man I just pretend like I'm not a working girl. That's what they want."

"I'm sorry you have to do this."

"Tis life, Brant. Don't tell me yer so naïve you think this is a choice. Now, are you gonna take me upstairs or should I look for business elsewhere?"

Brant smiled and shook his head. "I'm not looking for that. I just want some conversation. Sit here with me, talk, that's all I'm asking for and I'll pay you good."

"I do believe you're one of the good ones, Brant."

"So are you. Don't forget that."

So they pretended. He told her about his life on the ship, about his father and brother back home and she listened. She laughed in all the right places and took the coins as he slid them over. For just one night, Brant could pretend that he had someone waiting for him whenever he was out to sea, wanting to hear his stories of adventure. But when he made his way up to his room alone in the wee hours of the morning, reality came back. He was just a sailor, and he would grow old and alone like most of the men on the crew.

For the first time in his life, Brant began to wonder if maybe his father had been right… maybe this wasn't the life for him.

* * *

Brant barely noticed the passing of his twentieth birthday. Four years he'd sailed with the *BlackFox*. But this season was different from the others. If LaFleur had pushed harder than ever in the previous season, he was sitting back and relaxing this time around. It was the general consensus of the crew that he was getting tired. Soft. And there was talk that he wouldn't be captain for much longer.

It unsettled Brant to hear murmurs of discontent and mutiny ripple through the crew. He'd tried to talk LaFleur into following heavier trade routes. The men were restless, barely having enough raids to satisfactorily line their pockets with gold, and they were heading into the latter half of the season. And now, to make matters even better, LaFleur was talking about heading to Port Royale early and taking a longer break over the storm season. It was as if he was completely blind and deaf to the discontent spreading through his crew like wildfire.

He was getting old, tired. He'd spent too many years in a hard life and everyone saw it.

Brant was worried. He couldn't help but feel like a storm was brewing. And by the feel of things, the *BlackFox* wasn't going to get through it unscathed.

Brant woke up with a start as the sounds of running feet thundered overhead. That wasn't right. The men should all be asleep in their bunks. But instead they were up, which couldn't mean anything good.

He swung his legs out of his bunk and quickly pulled on his trousers and boots, grabbing his cutlass from where it hung on a peg on the wall. Refraining from running above, Brant walked cautiously up the stairs and peered out of the hold.

The deck was alight with lanterns and it seemed the entire crew was gathered on deck. Karl, LaFleur and Joseph made up a small group at the center of the foray. LaFleur looked as if he'd been roused from bed, his shirt untucked and barefoot, hair disheveled. But he looked anything but tired. His eyes were ablaze with anger.

Brant walked up on deck and joined the crowd of sailors to try to get a better idea of what was going on. The sick feeling in his gut told him to hang back, not to get involved, but he moved forward anyway; curiosity winning over.

"You're a bunch of cowards!" yelled LaFleur. "You drag a man out of bed in the middle of the night, for what? To betray him? To stab him in the back? You ain't happy with the way I'm running things, then you can leave at next port. That is how things work on *my* ship."

"Yer ship?" one of the younger sailors, Jacob, stepped forward. "This ship would be nothin' without us. You are nothin' without us. And quite frankly, yer draggin' us down."

Brant swallowed hard as the men around them yelled their approval at the apparent leader's words. He caught Karl's eye, silently asking what to do. All he got in response was a nearly imperceptible shake of the head. So he stood, his hand resting on the cutlass strapped to his hip and watching the crew members he called friends and family turn into crazed men. They were calling for blood, and he knew that this night would end with a red sun rising.

Shouts calling to throw him overboard, to maroon LaFleur, came from the men that were quickly taken up as a chant, rippling among the men like the words of dark magic. LaFleur was growing red in fury, and he pulled his pistol, waving it in the face of Jacob.

"Usurper! You're gonna hold a mutiny against me? I put food on the table and lined your pockets with gold!"

Karl reached for LaFleur's arm and rested his hand on his shoulder, whispering to their captain. *Calm down*, Brant prayed. He wanted to push his way through the crowd and join his captain. Instead, he stood on the outskirts, a coward, and watched the situation deteriorate before his eyes.

The minute LaFleur's pistol was waved in Jacob's face, Brant knew it was the end. The men were calling for blood. They'd lost faith in their captain and had elected a new leader. To lose control, like LaFleur was doing, was basically signing his own death warrant.

The chant for overboard had been dropped, and instead calls for a duel filled the ship deck. Though they were not calling for blood in as many words, they might as well have been. There was only one way a duel would end; in death, and Brant wasn't confident LaFleur would win.

Jacob drew his cutlass and turned to face the crowd of men that stood behind him. "A duel you say?"

"Yeah!" came the uproarious shout from the men.

"Winner be captain? No contest from no one else."

"Aye!"

Jacob turned to LaFleur. "What say you? Sounds fair to me. The men ain't happy with you, but they're willin' to give you a chance if you can best me."

LaFleur nodded. "Aye, tis fair."

Brant could no longer stand aside and watch. He pushed his way through the crowd. "Let me fight for you, act as champion," he called. He *knew* he could beat Jacob and secure LaFleur's captaincy.

But LaFleur and Karl shook their heads. "Nay, boy. You fighting for me won't help. I fight for my own place, or I hand it over."

LaFleur holstered his pistol and slowly drew his cutlass. "Clear some room!" he shouted.

Roars of approval erupted throughout the crew and Brant thought he might get sick. Karl grabbed his arm though, and dragged him to the outer edge of the large circle that was forming around the deck, leaving only Jacob and LaFleur standing, their blades glinting in the light of the flickering lanterns.

The fight began quickly, with clashing steel and the stomping boots of men as they picked up the beat of the fighting men.

Brant watched, fists clenched tightly at his side. He could see right from the start that LaFleur was outmatched, if not in skill, then age. He moved sluggishly compared to Jacob's robust youth as he deftly matched every step the captain made.

LaFleur was good with the blade. It moved like an extension of his arm, blocking Jacob's thrusts and slashes effortlessly, at first. But he was growing tired, slowing, while Jacob only pushed harder.

The fight seemed to have only just begun, when LaFleur stumbled. Brant reached for his sword, ready to leap to his aid, but Karl laid his hand on his arm to hold him back.

It happened quickly, but to Brant it seemed to move in slow motion, as Jacob lunged forward and his cutlass bit into LaFleur's stomach and protruded out his back. A dark stain slowly spread across his tunic and he fell to his knees. His face paled and lips turned an unnatural blue.

Brant tried to lunge forward, but Karl held his arm firmly. "No, boy. You ain't gonna do any good."

Slowly, Jacob pulled his blade from the fallen captain's stomach and turned his back to him, crimson betrayal dripping off the shining metal and onto the deck. He said nothing, walking away from the mess he had created and entering LaFleur's cabin. He'd made his point.

Once the cabin door shut, Karl let go of Brant's arm and he leapt forward, to LaFleur's side. He was lying on the deck, a pool of blood quickly surrounding him, but Brant didn't notice as he knelt in the warm liquid and held the dying man's hand.

"You don't do anything dumb now, you hear?" said LaFleur through sputters and chokes.

Brant shook his head. "This is wrong. They just turn on you, for what?"

"I got soft. You and Karl tried to warn me, but I was a fool."

Karl joined Brant at LaFleur's side, but he stood, stalwart and calm. He was no stranger to death.

LaFleur's breath grew shallow and his eyes fluttered, and Brant thought he had passed on until LaFleur squeezed his hand and his eyes opened again. "You keep my girl safe and well, you hear me? You keep her sailing strong."

A ragged breath ripped through his body, gurgling in his lungs as his soul clawed its way to freedom. Brant had never stopped to watch someone die. He'd always thought it was more peaceful and calm than this, despite the pain of injury that brought it about. Instead, the life tore out of LaFleur, escaping as his corporeal body fought to hold on. It was in man's nature to survive, it seemed that never went away, not even in the last moment of life.

LaFleur's jaw relaxed, open, as if shocked at his own mortality. His hand went limp in Brant's.

He didn't look up as Karl walked away. He held tightly to his fallen captain's hand. He wasn't a praying man. He'd never really been religious, but his mother had taught him to pray for the souls of those less fortunate, and her words came to him now. Silently, he mouthed the words that he hoped found their way to listening ears. "Lord, have mercy on his soul," he repeated over and over.

CHAPTER SIX

Brant clenched his fists tightly and took a deep breath. "Sir, we should take this route to Port Royale and unload. We're sitting low in the water and if a storm blows in—"

Jacob, the new captain, held up his hand. "We're not heading in yet. She's a good ship and she'll weather a storm."

He looked over at Karl, silently begging him for help, but he just shrugged. "Plot the course, Brant."

Brant sighed and collected his tools up from the desk that Jacob never should have been sitting behind, and walked out of the cabin, Karl following.

Depositing his tools on a table near the ship's wheel, he turned to Karl and threw up his hands. "He's going to have us all at the bottom of the ocean!"

Karl nodded, his face grim. "He's a fool and knows nothin' of running a ship. You see him after the last raid?"

He nodded. Jacob had celebrated with the crew members a little too hard, and had spent the entire day afterwards holed up in his cabin. No one had been allowed to disturb him except to bring him coffee and breakfast. The men had joked about how he was going soft, but if he kept this up it wouldn't be jokes for much longer. "He wants respect, but he doesn't want to give up his place among the crew."

"He don't start listening to someone, there'll be another mutiny before long. Mark my words."

The scary thing was; Karl was right. In the weeks since LaFleur's murder—that was what Brant had come to think of it as—Jacob had quickly showed his true colors. He was young, and green. He knew nothing of what it took to be a leader, or how to maintain control. He seemed to think he could order the crew around like his word was law, sit back and watch them do all the work, and then join in when it came to fun. In all his years serving under LaFleur, Brant had learned that as a captain you had to make certain sacrifices to differentiate yourself from the rest of the crew.

LaFleur would have a drink, maybe two, with his men. But he never overdid it and he always remained in control. He never asked more of his men than he was willing to give and he always pulled his own weight.

Jacob was riding high on power, refusing to listen to reason or advice. Brant and Karl had been patient with him, willing to help and offer advice, but he wanted nothing of it. It seemed like he had branded them traitors, followers of LaFleur, and didn't trust them.

Brant spread out his chart and began working on adjusting their course back into heavier trade routes. If Jacob wanted gold and blood, he'd get it. He only hoped that it wouldn't be the *BlackFox* that ended up washed red with the lost lives of men he called brothers.

Karl tapped his table a few times and clucked his tongue. Looking up, Brant raised his eyebrow. "Yes?"

"This island, you can bring us right by it?"

He looked at where Karl's finger was tapping and made a few quick calculations. "Yeah. Can we unload our hold there?"

Karl shook his head. "It be empty. Figure we keep it close by, just in case." He let out a sigh, like it was a great weight to let those words out, then tapped the chart one last time before walking away.

Brant frowned and looked back down at the map. Just in case. The way things were going it wasn't "just in case", it was just a matter of time.

***

Brant sat in the mess hall that night in silence, surrounded by men that had him both disappointed and feeling a little sick. They had willingly betrayed and murdered their captain, and now their murmurs of discontent were rising up again; this time against the man that they had put into power.

Their course had been altered to go near the island Karl had pointed out, but they wouldn't be near there for another week. Brant hoped things would hold together until then. Another mutiny would tear the crew apart. If LaFleur had three loyal followers, Jacob easily had close to half the crew, but the other half was growing more and more upset with his poor leadership. If it reached a boiling point, the *BlackFox* would be washed in blood, and no one would make it out unscathed.

A couple men sitting beside Brant were muttering angrily to each other as they ate stale bread dipped in stew.

"This swill ain't worthy of a dog," muttered one man, tossing the hard lump of crust aside. "We need to make port and stock up, and we ain't near no harbor."

The man beside him nodded. "Cap'n don't know what he's doing. Picking on the wrong ships. We ain't had a good raid even once this whole season."

Brant got up and took his empty bowl to the washing pot and deposited it there, then walked on deck. Karl was already up there, smoking his pipe in the cool evening air.

"'Tis calm," he said when Brant walked up to join him.

"Too calm. There's a storm brewing."

"Aye."

But he wasn't referring to the weather, and although it was calm out, the belly of the ship was simmering slowly into a boil. "We won't weather this one well."

Karl shook his head, puffing thoughtfully on his pipe as he stared out at the ocean. "One good raid, it'll calm things for a time."

"Long enough?"

Karl nodded.

"What if we don't get that raid?"

Karl smiled and pointed ahead. "Can't see her yet, but I saw a ship from the nest through the glass. She's sittin' low. We'll be on her tomorrow sometime."

Brant smiled slightly, but it was bitter sweet. He wasn't sure he could stomach more blood, but Karl was right; it would blow off enough steam to keep the men under control until they were in a better position.

"If a stray bullet found the captain…" he trailed off. He could end things tomorrow if they were in a raid. No one would notice that friendly fire had taken down their captain.

"There'll be a power struggle for who be captain. Best we let things be until the last possible moment, then take public action. Establish leadership."

Brant reached into his pocket and pulled out a cigarette, slightly bent and wrinkled. He lit it and inhaled the smoke. Karl was right, if he ended it during a raid, in secret, it would tear apart the crew more than any mutiny would. They had to be perfect in their timing, and act just at the point before boiling, when the men were good and ready to accept a leader who would present himself, but not quite ready to draw blood. The only problem was finding that perfect moment.

***

Karl was right, there was a raid the next day. But it didn't go as expected. Jacob was over eager, making the wrong calls at the wrong time, and refusing to take advice from the more seasoned sailors on his crew.

Brant took second watch that night. He wandered the deck, cigarette hanging from his lip and staring out at the water on all sides. He couldn't look down at the deck, still stained with the blood of crewmembers that shouldn't have been screaming in pain, dying, bleeding out on the deck boards of their home. The raid today had been a blood bath. They'd lost three men. Three! Three good men that shouldn't have been lost if Jacob had just let his pride go and allowed men with more experience advise him. There were another two in the infirmary. One had lost a leg, the other had a stab wound.

There had been no celebration tonight.

Jacob had tried to bring out the rum and start festivities, but the men had only somberly taken a swig, said a few words for their fallen mates, and passed the bottle off. Once it had made its rounds, the remainder was poured into the ocean, a kind of peace offering.

Maybe it was then that Jacob realized that he had made a mistake. One of his mates had pulled him aside, and since then Brant hadn't seen him. The glow of the oil lamp had shone from the captain's cabin window until well past midnight, but now in the wee hours of the morning it was dark and silent. Brant hoped his dreams were haunted by the blood on his hands, by the screams he had caused.

He hadn't had a chance to talk to Karl yet, but the fact that the raid had gone so badly meant they were short on time, and it was unlikely they'd make it to the island before things blew up. They had shared a look earlier, when the men had been paying their respects to their fallen comrades. He had seen the tired look in the old man's eyes, the look that said he was losing hope for the crew and ship.

"Hey, Foxton, yer off for the night, go get some shut eye," said Curly, a red-headed Scotsman who had found himself on the crew just last season.

"Thanks, Curly. Not sure I'll be able to sleep though."

The Scotsman clucked his tongue, but nodded. "Aye, I been tossing and turning myself. Yesterday don't sit well."

Brant nodded, but didn't encourage the conversation.

"Cap'n... he made some bad calls and a lot of the men are beginning to talk."

"Maybe the men should be content with who they put in charge," spat out Brant. It still didn't sit well with him how they had turned on LaFleur.

"Aye, you were close with LaFleur. I can't help but think we were better off with him, even if he was gettin' soft."

"You aren't the only one with that sentiment," muttered Brant, but he'd had enough of the conversation and he walked away, taking the ladder below deck where his bunk was waiting for him.

If men like Curly were beginning to come forward and speak openly of their unhappiness with Jacob, then they had less time than Brant had hoped. They were looking to recruit men to their cause, make sure sympathies lay in the right place. It wouldn't be long now. A ship was a small place and people knew where your allegiance lay pretty quickly. The question was; who was heading it all up, and when were they going to make their move?

Brant tossed and turned, true to his prediction, and drifted in and out of sleep. Any sleep he managed to get was full of nightmares, dreams of LaFleur bleeding out on the deck, dreams of him begging Brant to step forward and speak up on his behalf, to fight for him, to show his loyalty.

Brant hadn't slept well since the night of the mutiny. He'd been haunted by dreams and guilt. He knew LaFleur wasn't speaking to him from beyond the grave, blaming him for not speaking up, but he still felt the guilt weighing down on him.

He'd been voluntarily taking the second watch every night, usually tired enough by the end to catch a few hours of sleep before the day began. Today was different though. Perhaps it was the rising discontent among the crew that had the air electrified and dangerous—keeping Brant's mind too busy to consider sleep.

He rolled out of his bunk a half hour early, and pulled on his boots, walking up on deck. Curly was seated by the mast smoking, giving Brant a nod but not bothering to approach. Brant gave a nod back, and took the stairs to the upper deck where he found Karl, standing and staring at their wake.

Without a word, Brant started lowering the rope to measure how many knots they were traveling at. He did this three times a day; once first thing in the morning, once mid-day, and once in the evening.

"Curly approached me this morning," said Brant.

Karl nodded. "Things are deteriorating fast."

"We won't make it to the island."

Karl shook his head.

"I think we need to move, soon."

Karl nodded. He didn't seem to have many words this morning; he was somber, deep in thought. But Brant wished he would offer some kind of advice, the next step in their plan, because he was feeling a little lost and alone right now.

"Mayhaps we should just let things play out and find a new billet next port," offered Karl. It wasn't what Brant wanted to hear.

He wanted to yell at the man, scream at him that he was giving up, that LaFleur had charged them with making sure his ship kept sailing strong and proud, but he didn't. Maybe a part of him had been expecting Karl to back down. He wasn't young anymore; he didn't have the energy for politics and intrigue.

"You do what you feel is right," said Brant, finished measuring the knots. The rope lay coiled neatly at his feet, and he turned away to go make note of the time and speed in the ship's log.

Brant's ship's log was different from the captain's, and he kept it below deck in a small desk with his tools. When he went down to make his notes, the sleeping quarters were slowly stirring to life as men were getting up, stretching and pulling on their breeches and boots, but the good natured joking that should have been happening among the more lively bunch was missing. The crew was quiet, somber, reflective of Karl's own disposition, but there was a hum of danger in the air; like the rising humidity just before a storm.

Fine, if Karl wasn't going to give him guidance, if he wasn't going to fulfill LaFleur's dying wish, then Brant would have to take matters into his own hands. He filled in his log, then strode over to his bunk, grabbing his brace of pistols off his hook and strapping them on. He knew men were staring at him, but he didn't care. He drew one of his pistols, checked that it was loaded, and ran up on deck.

Bursting into the captain's cabin without so much as a knock, he was met with the sight of Jacob still asleep in bed.

It seemed fitting, that Brant drag this supplanter from his bed like he had done to the rightful captain.

Jacob slowly stirred, and looked at him in confusion. "What is the meaning of this?"

He said nothing, strode forward and grabbed the man by his shirt and forcefully yanked him from bed. He was deaf to Jacob's shouts of protest as he pulled him from the cabin and onto the deck, where a group of men had already gathered around.

"Prepare a boat," growled Brant to Curly, who was the closest. The man nodded, his eyes wide.

"What are you doing? You can't do this! I'm your captain!" shouted Jacob, but Brant ignored him.

"Listen up!" shouted Brant, calling attention from the angry captain he had clutched in his free hand. "A few weeks ago you all rose up against your rightful captain, and allowed this man to kill him in cold blood.

"You had it good. LaFleur looked after us; always made sure we had food in our bellies and gold in our coffers. But that wasn't enough for you. You ungrateful dogs wanted more, and you got this man.

"The ship has fallen apart quickly since he took over. I hear your whispers. I feel the discontent. You men would turn so quickly on a man *you* set in place? That *you* chose? Fine. You can't make up your mind, you would rather whisper treason and mutiny until it exploded in more blood, blood that still stains this deck from the deaths of our mates and captain? Then I will act for you."

Brant paused in his speech, looking around the faces of the men around him, and seeing shock unanimously registered in everyone's eyes.

"You all disgust me. You would see this ship torn apart on the reefs rather than sailing strong like she has for years. I can't allow that. I promised LaFleur I'd keep her sailing strong and proud, and I intend to do that.

"I won't kill this man you named *captain*," he spit out the title, dragging Jacob to the boat that was now extended beside the ship's rail, ready to be lowered. He pushed Jacob forward, and pointed his pistol at him.

"Climb in," he ground out through gritted teeth.

Jacob paled and climbed in without a word. His protests had grown silent during Brant's speech, and his eyes shone with fear.

"Someone collect his breeches and boots!"

Moments later a pair of breeches and boots joined Jacob in the small rowboat.

"Collect some water and food."

He held his gun steadily on the man, waiting for someone to bring what he had commanded. It didn't take long for a barrel of water to be rolled up and tossed into the boat, as well as a sack of various foods.

"Lower the boat," commanded Brant, his voice losing some of its anger.

Slowly the boat was lowered into the water below and he watched as the man who had killed his captain was sent away without even the slightest hint of protest from any member of the crew, even his mates.

Once he heard the tell-tale splosh of the boat hitting water, he holstered his pistol and then unbuckled the brace, holding it for everyone to see before tossing it over the rail to land in the boat with Jacob.

"I've done your dirty work for you to save this ship, but his blood, if he doesn't survive, is on your heads. Jacob is paying for his sins of mutiny against LaFleur, but don't any one of you forget that you all put him in that position and you are all to blame. Your malcontent and selfishness is to blame."

The crew stood silent for a while, and then murmurs began to rise up. "Who be captain now?" seemed to be the resounding question.

"We vote," said Karl, walking down from the upper deck where he had stood back through it all.

Brant looked at his friend, and the most respected man on this ship.

"Karl is right. No more blood will be shed because of leadership. Today, we continue on the course set. You talk amongst yourselves and at dinner we will nominate men for captain, then the crew will vote."

Nods of approval rippled through the crowd.

"Why wait for dinner?" shouted a crew member. "I nominate Brant."

Brant held up his hand and shook his head in protest. "No, it is only fair that we take time to think of nominations, and then vote."

Ripples of Brant's name went through the crowd until it was picked up by the entire crew. Brant's heart pounded. He didn't want this, he hadn't prepared for this. He had intended to nominate Karl, a much better choice for captain than himself. He was too young and inexperienced. But he couldn't deny the thrill that coursed through him; the idea that the crew wanted him as captain. His fingers were touching what he'd always wanted, and all he had to do was grasp it and it would be his.

A hand rested on his shoulder, and he turned to see Karl at his side. He held up his other hand and slowly the crew quieted.

"If it is unanimous that Brant Foxton be captain, then so be it. Otherwise we take nominations, and vote at dinner," shouted Karl, gaining everyone's attention.

The men all nodded and said their approval.

"Those who want Brant as captain, raise yer hand."

Brant watched, his breath caught in his throat as slowly arms were raised. He looked around at each man in the crowd. Everyone's hands were held high. He looked to his right, where Karl stood with his hand still rested on his shoulder, his other arm held high in the sky. There was no mistaking it; it was unanimous. He was captain of the *BlackFox*.

CHAPTER SEVEN

Brant looked nervously at the approaching ship. They had made port briefly after he had been elected captain—just long enough to stock up and empty their hold. Since then they had been out to sea for a month. Brant had taken this time to establish himself in his new role as captain, and had passed by most ships without even considering a raid. The men seemed understanding, allowing their new leader to learn the ropes, but they were starting to get restless and Karl had urged him that now was the time to make a raid.

"Run up the colors!" Brant called.

A cheer erupted from the men and feet stomped in approval.

The crew had given Brant respect, and seemed happy to help when he had questions, but he could tell they were beginning to doubt he had the metal to be captain. Waiting an entire month to raid a ship was pushing it, and he knew it.

Brant called Karl over and nervously clutched the railing. "Karl, I need you to lead this raid. Casper isn't ready to man the helm in this situation." What he really meant was he wasn't ready to lead his men into battle.

"You just do what you must and let me worry about the rest."

Brant nodded, relieved that he could stand back at a position he was more comfortable at, while Karl led the charge. Walking towards the wheel, he snapped his fingers and motioned Casper over.

"You aren't ready for this yet, Casper. You go take part in the raid."

"Yessir."

"Casper."

"Yes?"

"We've both had positions put upon us that we weren't ready for, but you're doing well and you'll make a fine Sailing Master."

"Thank you, Cap'n."

Casper left the helm and Brant took over. He would need all his strength and concentration to navigate his ship through the raid—his ship; it was only just beginning to sink in that this was his ship, he was captain, and he found a smile inching up his lips.

Karl shouted orders while Brant carefully steered his ship towards the other one, circling it and lining it up for a volley from the cannons. It was French, by appearance, and it looked like they were going to stand and fight instead of try to outrun them.

The guns were rolled out and Brant shuddered in anticipation. He loved the sound of the first cannon blast breaking the still that seemed to come over both crews just before a battle.

And then it came. The shouts of "Fire!" were screamed from both ships and the loud booms thundered through the air. Brant laughed and kept the *BlackFox* in line with the opposing ship, bracing himself for the impact of the heavy iron balls. As the ships drew closer and closer together, Brant could see the enemy ship beginning the flounder. Karl gave the orders to board, and then all hell broke loose. There was shouting and shooting and the clanging of metal on metal all mixed with screams of death. Brant itched to join in, but his job was to control the ship. He missed the rush that came with the chaos of a raid.

From where Brant was at the helm the whole thing seemed to go by quickly. Every once in a while he had to pull out his sword and fight off a sailor who had jumped over to the *BlackFox,* but it wasn't very often and he made quick work of it.

Karl came up to him when it was all over, and they dropped anchor while they took care of the ship, cleaning up and making any quick patches they needed to before sailing away.

"Should we give them quarter, sir?"

"Yes. There is no need to spill unnecessary blood. The ship is floundering anyway. Someone will hopefully come to aid them, but they won't be going anywhere in a hurry. Relieve them of their valuables and we'll be on our way."

Karl nodded and went to give instructions to the crew. Brant walked one of the planks that spanned the distance between the two ships and approached the prisoners who had been clustered in a group.

"Who's the captain?"

A man stepped forward and Brant sized him up; a typical French man who enjoyed frivolity a little too much.

"We will leave you and your men alive and with enough provisions for you to either make a port or get help."

The captain spit at Brant's feet. "You are nothing but a weak Englishman."

Brant smiled. "We shall see about that."

He walked away and went back to his ship where he briefed Casper on what heading to make, and then retired to his cabin where he could collect his thoughts and prepare for the celebrations that would ensue. In the past few seasons it had become tradition on the *BlackFox* for the men to have a bit of a celebration after their first successful raid of the year and, although not a first of the season, it was the first with Brant as captain and worthy of celebration.

He smiled as one of the men ran past his window and below deck—likely to pull out a crate of rum. He was jumping the gun a little, but as long as the anchor was pulled up and they were making headway, Brant didn't care if half his crew couldn't stand. There wouldn't be another raid today anyway.

* * *

Brant looked at Karl in shock. "What do you mean I'm wanted?"

"I mean, they want to put a pretty noose around your neck in Port Royale. It would be wise to adjust our heading and clear things up."

"Clear what up, exactly? And what happened to privateering status?"

"Apparently privateering status ain't transferable from cap'n to cap'n."

"So you're saying that when LaFleur died and I took over, I was acting illegally and am nothing more than a common pirate?" Brant could feel his blood pressure rising with every word spoken. He hadn't signed on for this. He'd wanted to serve the king, not himself.

"Aye."

"And you didn't tell me this, why?"

"I was as much in the dark as you, until now."

"There were no rules and bylines about this whole thing when LaFleur got into it originally?"

"Sure there was, I just didn't know."

"Who would I get a Letter of Marque from?"

Karl shrugged. "The Gov'nor, I suppose."

"Then we sail for Port Royale. We'll anchor off the coast, take a long boat in at night, and make a little visit to Governor Modyford."

"Very good, Cap'n."

"Karl—"

"Yessir?"

"Enough with the formalities; we both know I'm Brant to you."

"Aye, Brant."

"Thank you. And could you send Casper in?"

"Yessir."

Brant shook his head and laughed. Casper walked in moments later looking a little concerned. "Something wrong, Cap'n?"

"We need to make a change to our route and destination."

"Cap'n?"

"We need to head straight for Port Royale, but avoid other ships. No more raids. And we won't be making port."

"Sir?" Casper looked confused.

"Seems there's a price on my head," he offered in explanation. "Just change our course, and have us drop anchor off the coast, somewhere inconspicuous."

"I'll take care of it right away."

"Thank you. Oh, and Casper, try to get the shortest route possible. I don't like having a death sentence hanging over my head."

"Of course, Sir."

***

The winds seemed to be in their favor, pushing them towards Port Royale quickly. Brant didn't know if he should be thankful that he would be able to put this mess behind him sooner rather than later, or terrified that he was rushing towards a waiting noose.

They docked off the coast of Jamaica, near a small beach a short hike outside of the port city, and waited.

When darkness fell, Brant along with Karl and Christopher, lowered a long boat to the water below and rowed it the short distance to the beach. Hauling the boat onto the shore sufficiently high enough to avoid any incoming or outgoing tides, they double checked their pistols, and then set out on their hike through the dense jungle towards civilization.

It took a couple hours of pushing through brush and vines and walking dusty roads before they made it to the outskirts of the city. Walking down the streets, Brant knew they stuck out like a sore thumb, covered in dust and sweat, but they made their way to the good quarter of the city where Governor Modyford resided.

"Hey, you!" came a shout from behind, just as they were about to turn up a street where some of the more lavish houses were situated.

Brant spun to face the speaker and paled. It was a guard.

"Brant—" warned Karl.

"You and Christopher better get out of here."

Karl nodded, and he waved Christopher to follow him as they slipped into the shadows of a back alley, while Brant walked towards the guard.

"Can I help you?"

"What's your business around here?"

Brant shrugged. "Just out for an evening stroll."

The guard squinted at him in the low light. "You been drinking?"

"Not a drop."

"You're a captain?" asked the guard, indicating Brant's hat.

He grimaced. He should have removed his hat. "Yes sir, I am."

"What's your ship?"

His mind spun as he tried to come up with a lie, with a ship's name that wouldn't incriminate him, but for all the ships he knew and captains he was associated with, his mind refused to cooperate and offer him a name.

"You look familiar."

"I make port here quite often." Brant could feel the sweat pooling on his upper lip and forehead, and this time it wasn't from heat or exertion. "May I go? I'll head straight to my ship. I'm not going to cause any trouble."

The guard shook his head. "I think you'd better come with me."

Brant hesitated. Should he run? He knew Port Royale like the back of his hand and likely could hide, but that didn't solve his problem and he would still have to find a way out of the city. With a sigh, he nodded his acquiescence, unbuckling his belt which housed his pistols and cutlass, and handed it over to the guard who accepted it, then shackled Brant's hands.

As they walked through the streets towards what was undoubtedly the jail, Brant studied the guard's face, impassive and stony in the moonlight.

"Do you even know why you're bringing me in?"

"I saw a poster with your face on it. You're Brant Foxton."

So much for anonymity. He didn't reply; his silence was answer enough for the guard.

They approached the jail and the guard walked him to a dirty cell, which housed three other men. The smell that wafted out had Brant gagging, and thankful for an empty stomach.

"In you go."

Brant's eyes watered from the stench and his nostrils burned but he walked forward, and waited for the guard to release the shackles that held his hands firmly behind his back.

Once the door clanged shut behind him, Brant turned around to face the guard. "I want to see Governor Modyford as soon as possible. You tell him Brant Foxton, son of Calvin Foxton was brought in." Brant nearly choked on his father's name, the blow to his pride hitting him harder than any punch to the gut could. But this was a matter of life and death, and if it meant living to see many more sunrises, he'd put his pride aside just this once.

The guard smiled. "Yeah, I'm sure the governor will give pirate scum an audience."

"He'll give it to me."

"High and mighty, ain't you? Fine, I'll pass on the message, but don't expect much."

Brant nodded and turned away, finding a corner of straw to sit in, that looked somewhat clean, if there was even an inch in this cell that wasn't covered in filth. The other two men, his cell mates, watched him but remained silent.

Brant drifted in and out of sleep on the hard stone floor. Bugs and rats skittered about, waking him up frequently throughout the night. The stench was slowly becoming less noticeable as he acclimatized to his surroundings, but his skin crawled more with each passing minute. He itched constantly; convinced fleas were making their home on his person, and moved out of the straw, sitting on the cold stone where at least he could see what was moving along the floor instead of just rustling pieces of straw that had him wondering if it was the wind, his imagination, or a cockroach.

When the sun finally made its appearance, leaving a sliver a light through the tiny single window, Brant felt relief and energy flooding his body. He got up and started walking around, waiting for news that his message had gotten to the governor.

A guard brought breakfast, if the slop could really be called that, and the line of sunlight moved along the cell floor slowly, showing the passing hours. Still, no one came. He peeked out the window at the sun, and guessed it was nearing noon. When he finally heard footsteps echoing down the stone hall he walked over to the bars, eager.

"Brant Foxton?" asked the guard.

"Yes sir."

"The governor wants to see you."

The guard inserted a key into the door and opened it, motioning for Brant to turn around as he fished the shackles off his belt and locked them on Brant's wrists.

Leading him down the hall and out of the jail house, he was loaded into a wagon and driven across town where it stopped outside the ornate mansion that was known to all as the governor's house.

Brant was unceremoniously unloaded from the wagon and pushed into the house and a short distance into a dining room, where Governor Modyford sat, eating lunch.

"Unshackle him," he said, without looking up from the newspaper he was perusing.

The irons fell from Brant's wrist and he swung his arms around while twisting his wrists in little circles to get the blood flow back.

"Sit."

Brant pulled out a chair and sat down. The minute he relaxed into the chair a plate, set of cutlery, and wine glass was set in front of him. He took this as invitation to the food spread out on the table, and reached for various fruit, breads, and cheeses that were causing his mouth to water hungrily.

"Leave us," was the governor's last command as he folded his paper and set it aside.

Brant watched his host curiously while eating some grapes, waiting for the man to open up conversation.

They sat in silence for a time, Governor Modyford seemingly content to eat his lunch in peace and quiet before addressing the business at hand. Hungry, and the spread of fresh food too much to ignore, Brant feasted. He wasn't about to be hung now. He had the audience he wanted and he didn't plan on leaving in irons.

"So, Brant, you are Calvin's son." It wasn't a question.

Brant nodded around a mouthful of bread and cheese. "Yes sir," he said upon swallowing.

"And how did you find yourself in this line of… work?"

"I was a sailor on the privateering ship the *BlackFox*. It recently came under my command due to some unsavory circumstances, and I'm afraid I acted in ignorance when I raided enemy ships without a Letter of Marque."

"Unsavory circumstances?"

"Mutiny, Sir, of which I had no involvement."

"I see. And what is it you want me to do for you?"

Brant smiled, feeling more at ease with the situation by the minute. "I would like to pay my percentage to the king, and in turn we forget these piracy charges. A Letter of Marque would also go a long way."

Governor Modyford remained silent, sipping at his tea with a thoughtful look on his face. Finally, he set down his tea cup and looked at Brant. "You pay the required percentage and we will forget everything," he said. "And I'll commission the letter."

"Thank you, Sir."

"I'm doing this because you're Calvin Foxton's son. If you fall on the wrong side of the law again, don't expect any aid from me."

Brant nodded. "Of course, Sir, thank you."

The governor rang a bell and a guard came marching in, leaning in close to Modyford for instructions, and then leaving. Soon a servant came in with a small writing desk and set it by the governor, who turned to it and wrote up a letter, signing and stamping it, then sprinkling the wet ink with sand.

As he stood up to hand Brant the letter, he grasped his hand. "I take it you haven't heard of your father's well-being?"

He frowned. "No sir. Is he well?"

"He's been ill for some time, and news from London says they don't expect him to live out the year."

Brant took the letter from the governor's hand and nodded somberly.

"Thank you, Sir."

"I urge you to sail for England. If you leave now, you can beat the summer storms. No man should die without saying goodbye to his son."

Brant forced a grim smile and nodded, but couldn't bring himself to say anything in response. Maybe the governor was right, but Brant wasn't really Calvin's son anymore, and hadn't been in years.

He turned to walk out, pausing at the entrance way. "I'll have my men bring the gold this afternoon."

He walked out.

***

Brant left lunch assured of his future, but with a new weight pressing down heavily on his shoulders. He walked the five miles back to the beach where they had come in the night before. The long boat was no longer there, but the *BlackFox* was still anchored just off shore. He waved his arms for a few minutes, and then saw a long boat being lowered.

Karl and Christopher met him on the beach. "Everythin' taken care of?"

Brant nodded, but remained silent. Rowing back to the *BlackFox* he felt elated, but the news of his father's illness had him troubled. He hadn't intended to make any contact with his father, but now he was faced with his possible death and the unwanted feeling of responsibility for his younger brother, James. If Calvin died, he would have no one.

Back on the *BlackFox* he was greeted with cheers and pats on the back.

"We're back in business, boys. Let's make port."

"Brant?" Karl approached him as they sailed around the coast towards the harbor.

"Yes?"

"You okay?"

"Fine."

"What's the plan?"

"We sail for England with the morning tide."

CHAPTER EIGHT

The voyage to England was rough sailing. It was dangerously late in the season and storms were a growing concern. They weathered a couple large gales that had Brant wondering if he'd made a mistake, braving the treacherous seas this late in the year. But the *BlackFox* docked in London safe and sound, if a little worse for wear, in early June.

Upon docking and paying the required fees, Brant left the ship in Karl's care, rented a horse from the nearest livery, and rode towards his father's estate. It was a long ride, especially in the heat of the day, but Brant hardly noticed; his whole mind consumed by thoughts of his ill father. Was he too late? Would his father even agree to see him? Would James be bitter and angry towards him for leaving?

Riding up to the estate it looked the same as it did four years ago when he had left. Brant recognized a much older Markus walk out of the stables to meet him, and waved.

"Is that you, Master Brant?"

"It is, Markus. How have things been?"

"Not so good. You've heard about Sir Foxton?"

"I have."

"Doc says he ain't got much more time. You best go see him."

"Thank you, Markus. I rented the horse, is there any way we can arrange for him to get back to the livery? I think it is best I spend some time here."

"I'll see to it."

"Thank you."

Brant walked into the house, taking the steps leading up to it two at a time. He walked in with a bang of the door, the sound echoing through the large house and announcing his arrival to anyone who might be found inside.

He didn't have to wait long for the brisk, echoing footsteps to come from upstairs. James walked down the stairs and met his brother in the foyer. "Can I help you?"

Brant smiled a little. His brother held himself straight and tall, his arms clutched behind his back and wore a perfectly pressed and starched shirt and breeches. Not a speck of dirt could be found on him.

"How is father?"

"Brant?" James' face lost its impassiveness and was replaced with a hesitant grin.

"Who else?"

All semblance of propriety disappeared with a laugh and James jumped down the last few steps to embrace his estranged brother. "You're back! Are you staying for good? I missed you! Leo told me that you had left and that you were okay but when I asked when I'd see you again he said he didn't know."

Brant laughed at the bombardment of words and held up his hands to slow his brother down. "I'm here for a little while, I'm not sure how long yet. Now slow down and tell me how father is."

James face turned serious, and Brant had to smile a little at the series of emotions he was seeing pass over his brother's face in such a short span of time. "It isn't good, Brant. The doctor says he doesn't have much time left. I heard Markus talking, he isn't even sure how he's lasted this long."

"What is it?"

"Consumption is what he called it. The doctor said that sometimes people recover but it's extremely rare, and at father's age it seems to have hit him quite hard."

"Can I see him?"

"He has been asking about you—"

"Take me to him."

James led Brant up the stairs and into their father's room. "Father? There is someone here to see you."

"Who is it?" Calvin's voice had lost much of the strength it had once carried. Now it was raspy and weak from too much coughing.

"It's Brant, Father."

"Send him in."

Brant walked in and James shut the door behind him, staying out in the hall. Calvin Foxton was a shell of the man Brant had once known. His body looked weak and frail, his skin hanging loosely off his thin frame.

"So, my prodigal son has returned. Have you come to beg my forgiveness in hopes of getting my fortune while I lay on my deathbed?" He was taken over by a fit of coughing and Brant rushed over to help him sit up in bed.

"No, I came to say goodbye. I'm a captain now; I don't need anything from you."

"Is that supposed to impress me?"

"Four years, father. I left four years ago and I'm a captain. You are supposed to be proud."

"I'm dying; the last thing I care about is what you've accomplished. Nothing you say or do is going to change the fact that James is going to get every pound of the inheritance."

Brant grimaced. He hadn't come here for money, he'd come here to make things right, and yet his father could only think about what filled his coffers.

"I left. I never expected to be included in the inheritance after that."

"At least you aren't a complete fool."

"Calvin Foxton doesn't raise fools," spat out Brant, struggling to hold in his growing anger.

"And yet you threw away everything I gave you and chose the life of a common sailor."

"I never intended to be a common sailor. I'm a Foxton, and I had every intention of upholding that name as a captain of my own ship."

"And what do you do? Haul coffee and sugar?"

"In a sense, and anything else of value that I relieve a ship of."

"So you're a pirate, a common criminal."

"Privateer, actually."

Calvin Foxton was quiet for some time and then he looked at Brant. "You can stay here while you're in London if you wish. Now leave me be."

"Thank you, Father. I would like that very much." It took everything in Brant to remain quiet and civil with the bitter man lying in bed. From what he remembered of the prodigal son, he was welcomed home with feasting and joy. There would be no killing of the fatted calf for Brant.

Calvin lay back down and Brant left the room, joining James who was still waiting in the hall.

"I didn't hear any yelling."

"Can he still yell?"

James smiled sadly. "If he's angry enough. How was it?"

"Better than I expected. He invited me to stay here."

"Your room is all still the way you left it. Father told the maids not to touch it. He wasn't angry when you left, you know."

"What do you mean?" Brant asked, thinking back to the night he'd ridden away and the silhouette he'd seen standing in the window, watching him go.

"He was just sad. It was as if someone had died."

"You mean he didn't erase me from the family inheritance and prohibit the speaking of my name?"

"After two years or so his lawyer came over and I think he changed his will. To him you were dead. I remember him telling me that you weren't ever coming back and I think he truly believed that. We spoke of you sometimes, when I asked or when he was telling stories."

"Father told stories?"

"I think when you left he realized that he drove you away and he was afraid to lose me as well so he tried harder to be a real father."

It was strange for Brant to be having a real conversation with his brother. The last time he had seen him, James had been six years old. He was now ten and had matured a great amount. It pained Brant to see that he had missed so much of his brother's life.

"That is hard to believe; a kind Calvin Foxton," Brant said, followed by a chuckle that sounded bitter even to his own ears. "I thought he only knew how to command troops."

James laughed. "Oh, he is still like that, but he did try hard to get closer to me. He told stories and asked me what I wanted to do when I was older. He even showed me everything we owned and explained things to me."

Brant smiled, but it pained him to hear that his brother had gotten the father he had always wanted, always fought for. He could almost consider himself an orphan after his mother had died. "And now that he's ill?"

"He has me sit with him every day for a few hours and he goes over business with me. This house will be sold when he's gone, you know."

"Why?"

"Because that is what we thought would be best. I will go to a boy's school and this house would be empty. There is still the Jamaican sugar plantation."

"So you will go to one school and then the other until you're twenty, and then what?"

"And then I will either go to Jamaica to oversee the plantation or I will purchase a townhouse here."

"You and father have it all figured out."

"We do. His lawyer will look after the finances until I graduate. I will be given an allowance each week. Father doesn't want me, or our money, falling into the hands of a relative I barely know. This seemed like the best situation."

"Father thinks the best situation is for you to be independent at ten years of age? You're still so young, James. You're too young to have responsibilities like this, to have no parental figure other than teachers and a headmaster in school."

"It's what father thinks is best."

"What father thinks is best," Brant repeated the words that seemed all too familiar. "What do you want, James?"

"What father says is usually a good idea."

Brant shook his head, frustration mounting. "You need to learn to think for yourself."

James only laughed. "I suppose I'll have to pretty soon, won't I?"

His brother was becoming hard, like their father. Brant was sure he laughed and cried like a normal child, but James was completely at peace with the fact that their father was dying, that the big plan was for him to be completely alone in this cruel world. Everything should feel like it was crashing in on him, like it did to Brant, but instead he laughed it off as if it was just the circle of life in action.

* * *

During his time spent at home Brant had daily conversations with his father about what he had done with his life these past four years—more often than not his father would grunt in disapproval, but occasionally he expressed delight. Brant knew Calvin would never admit it but he was sure he secretly enjoyed hearing of Brant's adventures, because through them Calvin could relive his own glory days.

Brant was not invited or allowed to sit in on James' time with their father, as it was usually discussing affairs of the estate, of which he had no part of.

Time passed quickly for him, but every day when the doctor came to check in, he just shook his head and muttered something along the lines of "not long now."

As bitter as he was towards his childhood it pained him to see his father suffer with each passing day, yet he sat by his side and kept him company as long as he would allow. Sometimes his father would tell him tales of his glory years when his was a common sailor in the king's navy, working his way up the ranks. He had come from a middle class family that did not have a lot of money, but Calvin had worked incredibly hard in the navy and pulled a good wage as commodore. He saved his money, and as soon as he had enough he invested in a merchant company that dealt largely with the sugar, cotton, and coffee trades out of Jamaica. It was through that investment that Calvin grew interested in owning his own plantation in Jamaica. As he grew in favor with the king and the court Calvin suddenly found himself in a whole new class and had vowed that his children would have a better life. That was why he had refused to allow Brant to join the navy.

"Did you visit our plantation at all while you stayed over in Port Royale?"

"No, I didn't think I'd be welcome."

His father's face grew cloudy and Brant quickly changed the subject. "How is Leo?"

"I hear he is doing well. His father told me he settled in Jamaica to run their plantation a few years back. Such a shame that a young man with such promise would confine himself to that backwoods island, but the plantation is a good business."

"James tells me you plan on keeping the plantation, but selling this house."

"The plantation is a good source of income. James will be in school, so there will be no use for this house. When he is of age he can purchase a new one if he wishes to stay here."

"When summer is over, you understand that I must leave? James will have no one left."

"Yes, I understand you have a duty as captain to your crew. James and I have discussed all the arrangements that will be in place, you need not worry. Now leave me. I am tired."

Calvin ended their time of visitation abruptly, as he usually did when he was too exhausted to talk anymore. Brant just nodded and forced a tight smile.

"I'll bring you dinner later, Father," promised Brant as he left the room.

* * *

After Brant and James had eaten dinner that evening, Brant filled a plate and climbed the stairs to his father's room. He knocked before entering, but didn't wait for an answer. Quite often his father was asleep at this time, and Brant would leave the plate by his bedside for when he woke up. Tonight, however, Calvin was awake and sitting. Papers lay strewn about his bed and he seemed completely immersed in reading them.

"Is everything okay, Father?"

"Yes, yes." He sounded strong, stronger than he had since Brant had come home, though still far from his old self.

"Can I get you anything?"

"No, nothing. I just have a few things to go over."

"Alright, well here's your dinner."

"Put it on the night stand. My lawyer will be coming first thing in the morning so I would like breakfast at seven."

"I'll see to it that you get it."

"Thank you. Goodnight, Brant."

"Goodnight, Father."

Brant left the room, but he felt uneasy. He had seen men die before, he was no stranger to death and he had seen men become stronger in their last moments. Sometimes it would almost seem like they would pull through, and then a few hours later they would die.

He already knew his father would not survive. The doctor had said there was no hope, and Brant wasn't so naïve as to think he could be wrong. Seeing his father energetic and seemingly strong had him worried, and he couldn't help but feel a darkness descend on him. This could very well have been the last time he saw his father alive.

* * *

As morning dawned Brant was woken up by a scream. One of the maids came out of Calvin's room sobbing. He took one look at her and knew what had caused the commotion, but he had to see for himself. He went over to his father's bed and checked for a pulse. Nothing, as he had expected. James came running in then, his face ashen and eyes wide with fear.

"Is it father? What happened?"

Brant turned to face his younger brother, swallowing hard. "He's gone, James. I'm sorry."

James' face contorted in sorrow and tears filled his eyes, but he swiped them away angrily. "I'm sorry, I shouldn't be crying. I knew this was coming."

Brant went over to his brother and hugged him. "Our father died, it is right to grieve."

James nodded his head against his shoulder and allowed his tears to soak through Brant's nightshirt. He clung to him for a long time, sobbing, letting out emotion that Brant wished he could feel for his now dead father. Instead, he felt nothing.

"Let's get you out of this room. Markus will see to it that his body is looked after. The lawyer should be here shortly and we can attend to business."

"Yes, of course. I'll be in his study."

Brant called in the maid who was still standing in the hall sobbing. "Please, settle down. There is no need for this hysteria. I need you to take this breakfast back to the kitchen and then send for Markus to attend to the body. He will know what to do. Also, ask him to send for the coroner when he's done. It is not good for him to be here."

The girl nodded and ran off with the bowl of hot porridge in hand, tears still streaming down her face. Brant felt sorry for the girl, but there was much to be done and he had his brother to worry about. The maid would be fine, likely just shocked at finding a cold dead body.

He left his father's room and went to join James in the study where they would await the arrival of their father's lawyer.

* * *

Russell Johnson, Calvin Foxton's lawyer, looked too grave when he walked into the study and shook hands with Brant and James, as if putting on a show for the benefit of the grieving sons.

Sitting across the desk from Brant and James he began to pull out a few papers and lay them out.

"We had been preparing for some time for this day. Things are in order. This estate is in James' name, and I will arrange for it to be sold as your father requested. All the money will be held in a trust for James, of which he will receive a sum of twenty pounds per week as an allowance until he graduates, at which time the entire sum will be transferred to his name. Does this all seem satisfactory?"

The brothers nodded, so Russell continued. "Your father and I made a few changes to the will in the last couple weeks. First of all, James will no longer be inheriting the Jamaican sugar plantation, but I believe Calvin had discussed that with you already, James."

"And what will be happening to the plantation?" questioned Brant.

"Your father has decided that you, Brant, have inherited it."

He looked at Russell in shock and shook his head. "That cannot be right."

"It is. You can look over the paperwork yourself if you like, but his signature is on it. Call it the last sentimentality of a dying man. It is a thriving plantation that brings in a great deal of money; I would be happy with your inheritance. Now, there is something I have to discuss with Brant alone if you don't mind leaving us for a little while, James."

"Of course," said James, looking slightly concerned, but getting up and leaving the room without any question.

"Brant, your father sent me a letter a few days ago outlining some changes he wanted made. I was on my way over this morning to have him sign, but I'm afraid I was too late." Russell handed a letter over to him.

Brant carefully looked it over and then looked at the lawyer. "This means that my father wanted me to become the guardian of James?"

"Yes. There are a few guidelines though. When James turns sixteen he is to attend school here, in London until he is twenty, or some other school that you deem fit for a gentleman of his standing. You are also to spend summer every year either in London or at the sugar plantation. James is not to take part in any illegal activities and he must be given every opportunity to lead the life of a gentleman and a member of the king's court. Your father never signed the alterations so I can use this letter as his consent, or we can burn it and forget it ever existed."

Brant looked at the man and looked back at the letter. "I would like nothing more than to be my brother's guardian, but it's a choice he will have to make. I'll call him back in."

Brant called James back into the room and Russell Johnson once again explained the situation. James looked serious, much too serious for a ten year old.

"So I would live on Brant's ship, with him?"

"Yes."

"And I would still go to school?"

"That is correct. When you turn sixteen."

"If Brant doesn't mind, I very much like this arrangement."

"I would have it no other way."

"Then it is settled. I will arrange the liquidation of Calvin's possessions here in London and have the money wired to an account in Jamaica."

"That would be fine. I only have another few weeks before I leave London."

Russell got up from his chair and extended his hand first to Brant and then James. "I offer my deepest condolences to both of you. Calvin Foxton was a good man."

Brant thanked him and showed him out. He had a few weeks to arrange a funeral for his father, the uprooting of his brother, and the setting sail of his ship, and he wasn't sure he could handle it all. In fact he was quite sure he couldn't.

* * *

Calvin Foxton's funeral took place in a large church in the heart of London. It was well attended, treated like more of a social event than a time to mourn the loss of a decorated commodore. Brant and James heard enough well wishes and condolences and platitudes to make Brant feel sick. Everyone had something to say about what a great man Calvin Foxton was, and poor boys, having lost both parents. They must have forgotten that

James had never known his mother, and Brant had been missing from the family for the last four years. Women that Brant had never met in his life cried on his shoulder, expressing how much they would miss "dear Calvin" as he was such a good man and had given so much to his country. Brant wanted to know what he had given to his family.

Following the funeral Brant and James went back to their father's house where a small group of their father's friends came and had tea and cake with them. It was now that people finally began to acknowledge Brant's absence for the last four years. They asked him where he had been and what he was doing with his life. Most of them expressed disapproval for his chosen lifestyle, but a small few were interested and wanted to know more about the life of a privateer and how exactly he served the country. There was even one or two who commended him for his bravery and service, but they did so in hushed tones. Brant smiled and answered their questions as they came to the best of his ability.

The following week was spent entirely with Brant being pulled in two different directions. He was busy making arrangements for the departure of the *BlackFox* and preparing to uproot James and move him away from everything he knew.

James wanted to take everything with; his furniture, his bedding, every little thing that reminded him of home. Brant had to work hard to convince him to leave it behind and sell it. There would be furniture in Jamaica and anything else he needed could be purchased. In the end, James packed up a few trunks with his book collection and clothing.

Arranging to have his brother's things transferred to the *BlackFox*, Brant set James up with a bunk on his ship and took his leave to track down a blacksmith. He wanted to buy James a cutlass of his own—he would not have his brother defenceless on a privateering ship. The more he thought about it the more he realized that the *BlackFox* was no place for a ten-year-old boy who had been sheltered most of his life. His father had entrusted him with the well-being of his brother, and Brant would be exposing him to a dangerous and immoral lifestyle. He wasn't ready for this new responsibility. He barely knew how to look after himself and command a crew, how could he be expected to be a good parental figure? Calvin had the same experience as Brant, and his parenting had resulting in a bitter boy. The whole situation was quickly turning from overwhelming to terrifying.

Stepping into a blacksmith shop, Brant determined to concentrate on the task at hand: finding James a suitable cutlass.

"Can I help you?" asked a large sweaty man wearing a leather apron.

"I'm looking for a cutlass."

"Let's see what I have."

The man pulled out a few ornate blades which he presented to Brant.

He accepted each one at a time and tested their balance and took a few experimental swings and thrusts, but each time he shook his head.

"What is the best one you have?"

"It's nothing fancy."

"It doesn't have to be."

The man pulled out a relatively plain sword. The handle had beautiful metalwork, but it wasn't encrusted with any gems or inlaid with any gold. The blacksmith handed it to Brant, and he followed the same ritual as he had with the others.

"How much?"

"Thirty pounds."

Brant pulled out a bag and counted out the allotted money, handing it to the blacksmith.

Walking back to the ship, Brant carried his purchase proudly at his side. He had never gotten a gift for his brother, and he was looking forward to giving it to him. A boy's first sword was an important part in one's life—a rite of passage and a step closer to manhood.

Walking the ramp onto the *BlackFox,* Brant went in search of his brother who was likely trying to grasp the huge lifestyle change that was coming over him—especially after he saw his living quarters. He could remember quite fondly the first time he had seen where he would be sleeping. The *BlackFox* was outfitted with wooden bunks in the crew's quarters, but the beds were short and narrow and the mattresses made of straw that were refilled once a year for cleanliness reasons. That was not a common practice on most ships, but LaFleur had enforced it strictly and Brant had continued to do so. However, the beds were far from the standards of what James was used to. But Brant had gotten used to them and so would James.

Sure enough, Brant found James staring appallingly at the crew's quarters.

"I don't actually have to sleep here, do I? This is a joke, right?"

Brant laughed. "Would you rather sleep in the brig?"

"Does the brig have a softer bed?"

"No, it doesn't have a bed."

"And how long are we at sea?"

"Oh, a few months. We make various ports, but you and I will be remaining on the ship for the most part."

"And Karl doesn't have to sleep here? Or you?"

"Karl is the quartermaster and I am the captain. We have special privileges. I have something for you."

James looked at him in excitement, his distress over the sleeping arrangements apparently forgotten for the time being. "Really? What?"

Brant pulled out the sword with a flourish. "Your very own cutlass. I'll teach you how to use it."

James took the sword from Brant and turned it around in his hands. "Wow!"

"This is a weapon, not a toy. You must keep it sharp and clean at all times. If you ask some of the men, they'll show you how to look after it. If you don't do so, there are consequences. We have to always be ready to defend ourselves or fight others. You will not be taking part in any raids, but you will be held to the same standards as the other crew members. That means keeping your effects in good repair, you understand?"

James nodded furiously, a huge grin plastered on his face as he gripped the hilt of his brand new blade.

"Good. Then as cabin boy you can go report to Karl and he'll keep you busy until we cast off."

"Busy?"

"Chores, James. There aren't servants here to do your bidding. We have to do everything ourselves and everyone does their part."

"Oh."

Brant laughed at James' dejected face. "You'll get used to it."

CHAPTER NINE

Sure enough, James did get used to it and he quickly fit in amongst the crew. Brant took a walk down memory lane when he saw James emptying latrines and swabbing the deck; it hadn't been that long ago when those had been his daily chores.

The first few weeks the boy had awful blisters on his hands, but they soon callused and grew tough. James allowed his hair to grow long and his clothes became worn and dirty. Brant watched his younger brother transform before his eyes, from a spoiled young aristocrat into a hard working cabin boy. Money suddenly needed to be earned to put food on the table, and hard work made for a good night's sleep.

But, although James excelled at his new life of manual labor, he couldn't seem to pick up or even enjoy his daily exercises in swordsmanship. He didn't have the heart or desire to learn the deadly dance that was sparring, and Brant was quickly beginning to question his decision to take his brother on as a crew member. If he couldn't defend himself, he was better off living on the plantation with a tutor, where he could enjoy a life of luxury like he had been meant to. But he wasn't ready to allow his brother to waltz out of his life and be looked after by strangers, so he stayed and Brant continued to push him daily to learn and improve. Soon enough the boy would turn sixteen, and it would be back off to London and school for him.

"Can we stop for the day? I'm not very good at this," begged James as he let his cutlass drop uselessly at his side.

Brant did his best to hide his disappointment and nodded. "Of course, but you're doing just fine. It's an art form and it takes time to learn."

"Did it take you so long?"

Brant laughed. "It takes everyone a long time. I spent four years perfecting it, and I still spend every day trying to get better."

"But you're good. I heard the men talking; they say you're the best."

He walked away and stood at the railing, James following. "Who told you that?" He laughed.

"The men all say that's the case. Are you telling me it's not?"

"The men like to embellish things. You shouldn't believe everything they say."

"Why not? They have no reason to lie."

"They enjoy telling stories, James. It keeps life from being too boring. Now back to work if you don't want to continue lessons."

"All work and no play makes James a very dull boy," he chanted as he walked away to continue his daily chores.

"Karl!" called Brant as he walked up to the helm. Karl stood up from where he was mending a sail and followed Brant.

"Yes?"

"How long has it been since we've made a raid?"

"Three weeks."

"Are the men becoming restless?"

"They are, but they are also concerned for the young master Foxton's wellbeing. We had our first raid of the year and it scared him quite a bit."

"He said nothing to me."

Karl smiled. "Of course not. He wouldn't want to disappoint his older brother. He works so hard for your approval."

"This is our way of life. We need raids or we don't eat. James will have to get used to it."

"That is why you haven't been ordering raids either? We've passed a few ships in the past weeks, we coulda had any number of em. Who you trying to convince, me or yourself?"

Brant sighed. "I'm concerned about him too, but I'm also concerned about the state of this ship. It needs... work."

"Yer unsure of how to handle this." It wasn't a question.

"Yes! I have no idea what I'm supposed to do. I'm not a father, I'm a brother and I have no idea how to look after a ten-year-old boy. No idea at all. I have no idea if I should be sheltering him from my life, or allowing him to be a part of it. We're immoral men, Karl. Can we justify turning James into one as well? And who do I put first? James, or my crew?"

Karl shook his head. "There ain't no easy answer, and I can't tell you what to do. Your father entrusted James to you, so I assume he knew what kind of life he would be going into. You and I know we gotta keep this here ship afloat, so we have to either raid or find a new way to bring in money. Like you said, James will be fine. He'll get used to it."

"Thank you, Karl."

"Aye, Brant, tis why I'm here."

* * *

After Brant's talk with Karl he started ordering raids again, and despite the late start in the season the *BlackFox* docked in Port Royale with a hull full of pillaged goods. After a percentage was paid to the crown the rest was divided among the crew according to their rank. There was a little less than the men were used to, but none gave a word of complaint.

Brant and James prepared to go to their father's plantation. Brant hadn't been there for years, not since before his mother had died. He didn't have much memory of the estate, but found himself pleasantly surprised. The grounds were well kept and the house seemed in order.

Stepping into the house they were greeted by an older woman who introduced herself as Liza, the housekeeper. She was a single mother, her husband having died. Looking after the Foxton estate was a family affair for her; her son looked after the grounds and her daughter helped around the house, and was kept in pristine condition year-round despite the only inhabitants being the housekeeper and her children.

"I didn't know you'd be comin', Master Brant, or I would have had rooms prepared. I got news that Sir Foxton passed on, so sad. And this is your brother?" she went off on a nervous series of questions and statements.

"Yes, this is James. We'll be spending the storm season here and then heading back to sea."

"Back to London?"

"No, sailing—I am a captain. We'll likely spend most storm seasons here."

"Oh, it will be wonderful to have people living here again! I'll get Sarah to make you up some rooms and I'll get started on dinner. Will it just be the two of you?"

"Yes, thank you. You and your children are welcome to join us if you wish."

"Oh, we couldn't."

"Please do, it is much too large of a house for us not to eat and live together."

"Thank you, sir."

"I'll be in the study if you need me, going over the papers. If you see your son, could you ask him to let the foreman know that I am here and would like to meet with him tomorrow morning?"

"Yes sir."

"Thank you."

As Brant retired to the study he sent James to explore the grounds, of which there was plenty to explore. From what he remembered there was a stable—which had at one time been full of horses, but now more than likely sat abandoned. There was also a cricket field in the back and a patio. An expansive front yard with fruit trees and pathways completed the picturesque landscaping, and the two story Spanish plantation house was a work of art all on its own. The estate was cheery and bright, much different from the gothic architecture of the London home James and Brant had grown up in.

That night at dinner with Liza and her children; Sarah and Samuel, James asked Brant if he could have a horse.

"A horse? Whatever for?"

"It will give me something to do while we're here. There is so much to explore and it would be so much easier to do so on horseback."

"I'll see what I can do."

"If you want I can look around for a suitable horse for the master," offered Samuel.

"Thank you, that would be wonderful. I'm afraid I don't know much of animals. Just ships."

"We can't know everything, sir."

"Please, call me Brant."

Samuel smiled and nodded. "I went and spoke to the foreman for you today. He said he would be by the house tomorrow morning at seven. Is that good?"

"Perfect. What do you think of the man?"

Samuel blushed a little and looked down, obviously unused to having his opinion asked. "It's not my place to say—"

"I learned long ago that a smart man listens to the observations of those who see more than him. I'd like to have an idea of the man I'm meeting tomorrow."

"I think he is good at what he does but perhaps a bit more harsh than necessary. But the men always pull a good crop."

Brant frowned. He didn't believe that a strong hand was always best, and if Samuel was right in saying the foreman was harsh there would likely be some changes made in the near future, but for now Brant's main concern was becoming acquainted with the plantation and everything involved.

"Would you be able to give me a tour of the plantation tomorrow afternoon?"

"Of course. It is best done on horseback, but my mother and I each have a horse here that we can make use of."

After dinner Brant locked himself in the study again to continue looking over the books. Pouring himself a glass of port, he sighed and smoothed out the page he was looking at. Not for the first time today, he wished he had paid more attention in class for the short time he'd attended school. It should be a simple task, to figure out where they stood financially. If there was a deficit or a surplus and why, but nothing was simple when what you were looking at looked like a different language.

* * *

Summer on the Foxton estate was different from any other Brant had experienced in Jamaica. He enjoyed watching James return to his childlike innocence. He had noticed that even the ten months on a ship had caused his brother to harden. It went fast when you were surrounded by men who made their living by killing and stealing

It was hot in Jamaica, that was nothing new to Brant, but it was to James who was used to overcast and rainy England. Most days he ran around wearing next to nothing but his breeches. Brant just laughed and enjoyed Liza's expression of horror. She had quickly adopted James and fussed over him nonstop when he was anywhere near the house—much to

James' dismay. When storms rolled in, they closed themselves indoors and waited out the weather with games and reading. Brant had a family. Gaining command of the *BlackFox* had given him a sense of accomplishment, but having James back in his life had him feeling like he was starting to put his life together.

This summer, unlike all the others, went quickly, and although he was ready to set sail, Brant left the estate with a sense of loss. The men however, were eager to set sail after a summer of being land locked. Even James was excited to return, evidently the thought of having Liza as a caretaker was more terrifying than swabbing decks and cleaning latrines.

Leaving Port Royale, Brant watched the disappearing shore line and smiled. That island was as close to home as he ever got on land, but he was always happy to be back on his beloved ship, back on his beloved ocean.

* * *

James burst into Brant's cabin, hair disheveled, not even pausing to knock or request permission to enter. Brant was sitting at his desk looking at charts and maps.

"James what have I told you about knocking?" he asked, not looking up.

"We have a problem."

Brant glanced up, and at the sight of his brother's concerned face, gave him his full attention. "What do you mean we have a problem?"

"On deck."

Getting up immediately, his chair tipping back precariously before settling back on all four legs, Brant strapped on his cutlass and brace of pistols, following James on deck where he saw the crew standing at the rail, all looking in one direction.

"What in blue blazes is going on?"

Everyone looked at Brant, but no one responded. "Well? Karl?"

"It seems we're about to come under attack."

"By whom?"

"A pirate ship, Cap'n."

Brant frowned. "Who is it?"

"Looks to be the *SeaVulture*. Ol' Richard's ship. He's a nasty sort; known for preying on other pirate ships and takin' all their booty."

Brant almost smiled when Karl referred to their spoils as booty, but he was more concerned about this Old Richard than any of Karl's quirky words.

"We can outrun him."

"Aye, we can. Should I give the orders?"

Brant pulled out his eyeglass and shook his head. "No, run up the colors. We won't be run off by a lowlife pirate."

"Brant," Karl replied hesitantly. "Ol' Richard is known for his cruelty. He will give no quarter if we fall."

"The men can handle it."

"You sure?"

"Give the orders."

Karl nodded and walked away shouting at the men. "Get yer lazy asses to work! Enough lolly gaggin! Run up the colors! Run out the guns! Casper, get yer no good sailor's butt up to that helm and steer this ship, for goodness sake! Did ya forget yer job?!"

"Brant?"

"Yes, James?"

James had been standing next to Brant and Karl the whole time, silently listening to the exchange.

"This fight is going to be different, isn't it?"

"These men are very dangerous and do not have honor like the ships we usually attack. If we fail I want you to jump overboard. You can swim, right?"

"Markus used to take me to the swimming hole in the summer."

"Good. You will go hide below deck but if any strange men start coming down you find a way off the ship. You find a way overboard."

"Why overboard?"

"Because, if you pretend to be dead in the water they won't touch you. Just jump in and lie on a piece of wreckage perfectly still. Can you do that?"

"Yes sir."

"That's a good boy. Now go below deck before the fun begins." Brant smiled a wickedly mischievous smile. As much as he hated the killing aspect of it all, he loved the rush of the fight, and this pirate ship deserved every bit of what was coming from Brant and his men.

"Sir, we're coming up starboard side. Should I give the orders?" asked Karl.

Brant watched the *SeaVulture* make its way up beside the *BlackFox* and gave a nod.

Karl turned to the men lined up on the thirty-six cannons the *BlackFox* boasted. "Fire all cannons!"

The thunderous roar filled Brant's ears and he smiled. The deck shook beneath his feet, but he could see the *SeaVulture* was under gunned and they just wanted to get close enough to board. That was their game.

"Casper, don't let them get too close. I want to hurt them, then we'll make a run for it. That should be enough to get the message across."

"Aye sir!"

Karl turned to look at Brant. "We aren't boarding?"

"No. The risk is too high."

"Aye, I think that be wise."

Brant watched the continuing battle, but it wasn't long before it was over. The *SeaVulture* saw they couldn't inflict enough damage with their lack of firepower, and there was no way they were getting close enough to board. So with little options left, they turned tail and limped away.

"Should we give chase, Cap'n?"

"Let them go."

* * *

It wasn't long before they crossed paths with the *SeaVulture* again. This time it was pillaging another ship. It was barely afloat and it looked as if Old Richard and his crew had just finished off, and as the *BlackFox* came into view they raised anchor and left.

"There won't be anything left there for us, Cap'n," said Joseph, ready to move on to more promising prospects.

"We'll board anyway. Search for survivors."

Getting as close as they dared, unsure if it was a trap or not, they dropped anchor and a small boarding crew that consisted of Brant, Karl, Joseph, Harold, Christopher, and Geoffrey took a longboat to see what was left. Climbing up a small ladder, they wandered around the destroyed ship. The deck was littered with bodies of men sporting uniforms of the British navy. But the most profound thing was that it was silent, absolutely and utterly silent. Not a single groan of an injured or dying man. Just silence. There was no one left alive in all the carnage.

"Search the hold, cabins, crew's quarters, every inch for someone who might be hiding. This ship won't stay afloat long," commanded Brant, unable to tear his eyes away from the sight before him.

The men fanned out, leaving Brant to search the dining room, state room and captain's cabin. Brant tried the captain's cabin first but didn't expect to find anything, nothing alive anyway.

The captain was dead in the middle of the room, as were a few men that lacked the presence of a uniform—likely Old Richard's men. At least the man had put up a good fight.

Leaving the cabin, Brant skipped the dining room and entered the state room. If the ship was carrying passengers, they would have been situated here. It had been completely pillaged but it was apparent that the passenger had been a woman. He paled at the thought of what could have happened to her. He was about to turn and leave but the sound of something rustling and a muffled gasp had him pause.

"Hello?" he paused. "Anyone in here? I mean you no harm. I am a servant of his Majesty the King."

"If you are a servant of his Majesty then why do you dress like a common pirate?" a woman's voice sounded from under the bed.

Brant quickly strode over and crouched down, looking under the torn and ripped mattress, making eye contact with a pretty young blonde. "I am a privateer, ma'am. This ship will sink soon, so if you would allow me to assist you, I can take you back to my ship and return you to a British outpost."

The girl shimmied out from under the bed and drew herself to full height, smoothing down her skirts and patting her disheveled hair. She was tall, thin and held her head high, lacking nothing in self-confidence. "My name is Catherine Marshall, and I would be very much in your debt if you would take me to England. I can pay passage."

Brant bowed low. "*Captain* Brant Foxton. We will discuss the matter of passage later."

"Thank you, Captain Foxton. If you don't mind I will try to collect a few necessities from what those thieves left and I will join you on deck momentarily."

"Of course, Miss Marshall."

Brant left the state room and waited for Catherine on deck. His men were already gathered near the rail, a boy, heavily wounded, lay on a makeshift stretcher among them.

"Is this all?"

"Yes, Cap'n. We couldn't find any others. This one has a pulse, but he's passed out. The doc will have to take a look at him, but I don't have much hope."

"I found the passenger—she'll be joining us momentarily. You best load that poor boy into the longboat while I wait for her."

It was long and laborious work, but between the five of them they had the nameless sailor lying comfortably in the bottom of the long boat.

Catherine soon joined Brant on deck and he helped her down the ladder and into the longboat. She hadn't been able to collect much—whatever had been left had been ruined, but Brant assured her that he had some things in the hold she could go through.

She didn't speak to the crew at all and they didn't attempt to approach her. She sat with such an air of self-importance—her petite little nose held high in the air—that she was completely unapproachable. Brant chuckled as he watched her, and was met by a slight frown. So, he could break through her pristine exterior after all. They had a good two months voyage to England and he couldn't help but think that it would get very interesting unless she learned to relax.

Arriving back at the *BlackFox*, Brant helped Catherine up the ladder, and then men lowered ropes to tie on each corner of the stretcher so that they could slowly raise the injured sailor up.

"James, go tell the doc he has a patient," instructed Brant as he led Catherine to his cabin. "I'm afraid it's a small ship and doesn't have a state room, so you can take my cabin. We do however, have a dining room that I and my higher ranking crew members dine in, and you're more than welcome to join us. I promise they are perfect gentlemen.

"You are a guest among us and are free to wander around as you see fit, but please try to stay out of the men's way when they are at work."

"Thank you very much, Captain."

"My pleasure, Miss Marshall. If you need anything please feel free to ask anyone as they will help you as best they can. And I must apologize in advance, but I may need to make use of my cabin from time to time as my desk and effects are all kept here, but I promise I will do my very best not to invade your privacy."

"Please, don't trouble yourself over it, Captain. I'm very grateful to you for helping me."

Brant left Catherine alone in his cabin and he went to speak with Karl. "Burn the ship," he said as he approached his quarter master.

"Sir?"

"Burn that ship and then have Casper change our course to London."

"Yes sir."

"Is the doc looking at the boy?"

"Aye, but I've heard nothing of his condition."

Brant nodded, he hadn't expected anything more. "I'm afraid I'll have to take your cabin for the time being. Are you okay in the crew's quarters?"

"Aye."

"Have someone come get me when the doc knows more."

"Brant, can we afford to take on a passenger all the way to England? We can't go about our raids with the lady aboard. It wouldn't be safe for her, and it could be dangerous for us as well. The only thing standing between us and a noose is that letter of marque, and if she reports bad conduct—"

Brant smiled slightly. "She's a lady of the court, Karl. She'll pay passage. It'll be a tight year, but it's early enough that I believe we can make it back to Port Royale before the worst of the storms roll in. We'll get a few raids in then, enough to keep the men happy."

"Pickings are gonna be slim that time of year."

"I know. But what do you want me to do about it? Leave her out here?"

"No, but we can dock at the nearest British controlled island and leave her with the governor. He can arrange to get her home. It will take less time, Brant."

"I need to see her safely back."

"Confounded chivalry—"

"That'll be enough, Karl. If you wish to question my decision please speak to me later. We have an audience."

Many of the men had stopped what they were going about to look at their captain and quarter master and it didn't sit well with Brant to have such an obvious and public questioning of his authority. He always allowed Karl to speak freely because he had experience and years that Brant did not, but this was too much. "I need to keep the men's respect, Karl. You are not helping. Now, can you respect my decision?"

"Ach! Brant you always gotta help people, but I think tis gonna make it a hard winter for us is all. But yer the Cap'n. You make the decisions and aye, I'll stand by you."

"Thank you."

Brant walked away feeling troubled. It was not often Karl spoke up so vehemently against an order, and it had him concerned. Was he going soft? He had a responsibility to his crew to make sure they were fed and provided for as well as had money to get them through the summer. Was he abandoning that responsibility by going to England? Brant shook his head. No. If the men didn't get enough, Brant would pay them from his own pocket. He could afford to do so with his thriving sugar plantation. He had a good crew and he wouldn't risk losing them, but he also had a sense of honor and he needed to see Catherine Marshall home safely.

* * *

Catherine stayed in her cabin for the remainder of the day until she became hungry and decided to venture out and find something to sustain her. She didn't have to go very far before she ran into a young boy who gave her a charming smile.

"Hello, Miss Marshall. Captain Foxton has asked me to invite you to join him and his men for dinner. They're in the dining room."

"Thank you."

She didn't give the boy a second look or thought. He was grubby, a mere cabin boy, and she fully intended to keep her contact with the crew members to a minimum.

Catherine entered the dining room, and the men all stood up around the table. The captain pulled out a chair for her to his right and she seated herself, observing the array of food on the table. It was mostly all things that would keep for some time; potatoes, salted meat and a few pieces of fruit that they must have picked up in their last port.

The captain seemed quite young to have his own ship. He was also well mannered and educated. Where had he come from? And what story did his life tell? He was quite obviously not of the King's navy and he had admitted earlier to being a privateer, but it was strange for someone of good breeding to choose this life, and he was obviously of good breeding by the way he spoke and held himself.

Catherine ate her food in silence unless addressed directly and concentrated very hard on ignoring the overbearing meaty taste of the salted pork. On any normal occasion she wouldn't have touched it, but Catherine was also raised better than to refuse food, and even in the company of a bunch of sailors she would not allow her manners to fall to the wayside.

The captain was jovial with his crew. He laughed and teased and asked their advice on matters. He was by far the youngest man in the room, with the possible exception of the sailing master, Casper.

As dinner drew to a close, the men left one by one until the only ones remaining were Captain Foxton and his quarter master, Karl.

"Did you enjoy dinner, Miss Marshall?" asked the captain.

"Very much, thank you."

"And is there anything we can do for you or get for you before we retire for the evening?"

Catherine glanced at the small windup clock on the wall and was shocked to see it was nearing ten o'clock. "No, thank you. I would like to get some changes of clothes tomorrow if that's possible. You mentioned you might have some in your cargo."

"Yes, of course. We'll take care of that in the morning."

Catherine smiled and stood up, politely wished them a good night and made her way back to the cabin she was borrowing from the captain.

* * *

"Any news on the boy we took to the doc?" asked Brant after Catherine had left.

Karl shook his head. "No. Doc stitched him up as best he could, but only time will tell if he'll pull through. He needs to wake up."

"And if he doesn't?"

"If infection don't set in I think he'll be fine, but I ain't no doc."

Brant nodded. "There aren't many men I hate, and I know some pretty questionable characters, but Old Richard is some low life scum that I wish I could rid the world of."

"Yer mad about the boy? Tis just the business of things. You've killed boys too."

Brant shook his head. "No. I'm mad about the lady. What would have happened to her if they had found her?"

Karl shrugged. "She was only shaken up a bit. No real harm done in the end. Everything they ruined of hers she can probably afford to replace ten times over. Don't you go pickin' fights you shouldn't be."

"But you don't like Old Richard either."

"No one has a liking for Old Richard, but he be a ruthless one. Don't get involved, Brant."

"I'm not going to hunt the man, but if he ever happens to cross my path I'm not going to let him run away with his tail between his legs."

"You best not hunt him," Karl warned, standing up and leaving the room.

Brant leaned back in his chair, balancing it on the back two legs while throwing his booted feet up on the table. Closing his eyes, he listened to the creaking timbers of the ship and the slapping of the waves on the hull. It was a peaceful night. One of the men on watch was playing a harmonica and the haunting tune floated in to greet Brant's ears. He sighed and sat there for nearly an hour listening to everything and nothing. Resting the chair down on all four legs, he got up and snuffed out the lanterns around the dining area before walking back on deck where he climbed up to the crow's nest.

He came up here when he wanted to be alone and to think. He thought about how his life had progressed in the six years since he had left home. It was hard to believe that he had managed to work his way up from a nothing cabin boy to a captain in five years, and now he had his younger brother to raise, which was an enormous responsibility, one that he struggled with every waking moment of every day. Brant often toyed with the idea of leaving this life behind and starting a family of his own while giving James a proper life, but every time he started thinking about it he realized what a hold the ocean had on him. There was no way he could ever leave this life, and he couldn't bring himself to begin a family when he would never be around. He had vowed long ago that he would be a better father than his had been if he ever had the opportunity to have a wife and children. Right now it was completely out of the question. Children aside, where would he ever find a woman who could love him for who he was and what he did? Not that he was overly interested in women right now. His life was complicated enough as it was, and a woman only ever succeeded in complicating things more.

Brant casually looked over the edge of the crow's nest down towards the deck, and saw the two men who were on watch leaning against the mast and conversing quietly. He smiled and looked over towards the steps that led to the hold, crew's quarters, officer's quarters, galley and even a small room for the doc. It was a small, cramped ship but it served its purpose well. It carried a crew of about seventy men, all hardy, well trained, and efficient killers. The ship doctor walked out from the stairwell and leaned against the starboard side railing, lighting a pipe. Brant decided it was time to leave his thoughts behind and climbed down to talk to him.

"Hello, Doc."

"Cap'n."

"How is the patient doing?"

The doctor puffed on his pipe a few times and then shook his head. "He's awake but in pain. There isn't much to be done but keep the wound clean and hope that he's a fighter. It's a stomach wound, Cap'n. Those are bad things to get. Infection builds up easily and it's hard to fight."

"Is he well enough for me to see him?"

"It can't do any harm."

Brant left the doctor alone to smoke his pipe and walked down into the cramped doctor's quarters that held the man's bed and belongings as well as an operating table and everything else he would need for his profession.

A groan came from the patient, and Brant walked over to him and sat down on the small stool placed next to the bed.

"How are you feeling?"

"Like bloody hell. Doc said I got my innards ripped up pretty good."

Brant smiled slightly. "It looks to be that way, but you aren't dead yet so you're a fighter. You'll make it through. How old are you?"

"Fifteen, sir."

"And at fifteen what exactly were you doing on a ship belonging to the royal navy? It's not like you could have completed training."

"No sir. I'm a civilian. I was apprenticing under the sailing master."

"Are you a mate yet?"

"No sir. I barely started my training."

"And what's your name?"

"Matthew, sir, but everyone calls me Matt."

"Matt, I'm Captain Brant Foxton and you're aboard the *BlackFox*. We are currently en route to England to bring a passenger home. You will be looked after as best we can, and I assure you our doctor is very good. Please do not fret about anything as we are more than happy to feed and clothe you. Your only job is to get better."

The boy smiled and Brant thought he would have laughed a little if he hadn't been in so much pain.

"Now you rest up. I'll send someone to visit you tomorrow."

CHAPTER TEN

Catherine was a late riser, and when she finally made an appearance on deck the next day it was well into the afternoon. James had knocked on her cabin door with a breakfast tray, but when there had been no answer he'd just slipped it inside and closed the door behind him.

"Good afternoon, m'lady. Nice of you to finally join us," teased Brant.

Catherine didn't seem in the least bit phased. "Breakfast was a bit cold. I'd prefer to have it brought at 9 AM."

Brant raised an eyebrow. "We'll see."

"Now, I believe you mentioned something about clothes yesterday."

Brant nodded then waved James over. "Go visit that sailor, Matthew, in the infirmary. I'm sure he'd enjoy some company."

Catherine tapped her foot impatiently.

"Yes?"

"Clothes. I'd like something fresh to wear."

"Right this way, m'lady."

Brant led her below deck, and indicated some trunks she could rifle through. He watched her as she looked through dresses, breeches, and shirts. Every one she picked up, inspected, and then put aside. Karl was right; he should drop her off at the nearest British settlement and let the governor deal with her. She was stuck up and arrogant and treated him as if he was beneath her, scum. That didn't sit well with him. He had been born into a family name just as good as hers, and just because he chose to do actual labor for a living did not make him inferior.

"Is there a problem with the clothes?"

"These are all stolen."

"And here for you to use as you please. You need clothes do you not?"

"I'm wearing clothes right now," she responded quite matter-of-factly.

Brant smirked and looked at her steadily. "A few minutes ago you were in a hurry to get something clean and fresh on, now you're content to wear that same get up for the entire two month voyage?"

"If I must."

"I'll happily keep them as they're worth some money, but I'll give you one last chance to choose something before I retract my offer."

Catherine shot Brant a glare and "humphed" quite childishly. Brant had to bite his tongue to keep from laughing, and instead looked at her smirking, trying to contain his amusement.

"Very well, I suppose I have little choice in the matter as clothing is a necessity."

"Well, some of the crew may think that it is optional, but I would very much suggest that you don't follow that way of thinking. Also, might I suggest you choose some simple things? A ship really isn't any place to show off your taste in fashion."

"I'll wear whatever I wish. Thank you, Captain."

"As you wish, Lady Catherine."

"That's Lady *Marshall* to you." She drew herself up to full height and steadily returned Brant's gaze.

"Of course. Are you done here then?" he asked looking pointedly at the small mound of clothing in her arms."

"Yes." Catherine, ever polite, forced a smile and walked with a purpose past Brant and up the steep set of stairs to the main deck.

Brant chuckled in amusement and casually followed his passenger. "You know you should be a little kinder to your rescuers," he said as he caught up with her.

"I have been perfectly polite."

"I'm not talking about polite. I'm talking about getting your pretty little nose out of the air and acting as if we're humans, not the scum of the earth."

Catherine threw her clothes down on the floor of her cabin, or rather his cabin, and turned to face him angrily. "If I treat you as such it is because you are. You're nothing more than a criminal who deserves to be hung and the same goes for every man on this ship."

Brant's eyes flashed with a fury he hadn't experienced before. No one had ever told him he deserved to die and if it had been anyone other than the high and mighty Catherine Marshall he would have challenged her to a duel to defend his honor. Which, despite being a privateer, he had plenty of. "You wish me dead then?"

"I wish all men of your profession dead. You give the British a bad name."

"We fight for our King. We risk our lives so that you can attend all your frivolous parties without worry that harm will befall you. We keep the Spanish, the French, the Dutch, or whoever else said the wrong thing at bay. We keep them just poor enough and just weak enough that they wouldn't dare declare war."

"You cause aggravation among the countries that are already near the boiling point."

"And what do you know of politics, sitting in your cozy and luxurious parlors sipping tea and doing cross stitch?"

"I resent that comment, Captain."

"You have your opinions and I have mine. I would like to know where you come off being so high and mighty."

"High and mighty? I know more about politics than you do, I'm sure. My father is the British ambassador to Spain, and quite often I go with him on his trips there. I know more about the volatile state of Spain than you or many other men do, but since I'm a woman I'm brushed aside."

"I would not discount you due to your gender, but when you come onto my ship and look down your nose at me and my men it gives me the impression that you are horribly naïve."

"Get out of my cabin."

"I'm sorry?"

"I said get out. You are incredibly rude, Captain Foxton, and I will not stand for that. Get out."

"This is my cabin which I'm letting you use out of the kindness of my heart."

"I don't care. Get out."

Brant threw up his hands in frustration and stalked out of the cabin, slamming the door loudly behind him. When he stopped to collect his thoughts, he looked around and noticed the stares of his crew members.

"What are you looking at? Back to work!" Brant ordered as he angrily made his way up to the crow's nest, sitting there for only a few minutes before he was joined by Karl.

"Might there be a good reason yer stompin' around and slammin' doors like a child?"

"She infuriates me. She said we all deserve to hang and then she ordered me out of my own cabin."

Karl chuckled. "And did you provoke her?"

"I asked her to be a little less pretentious towards us."

"I see. Well that just be women. Ignore her or she'll think she can get your goat whenever she pleases."

"Karl... She's just... Why did I ever take her onto my ship?"

"Because yer a good man. Now stop bein' childish and start bein' captain."

Brant sighed and nodded, following Karl down the mast and to the main deck.

* * *

Later that evening Brant went to visit the injured boy, Matthew. He had allowed James to get out of most of his chores so that he could spend time with Matthew, entertaining and keeping an eye on him. A stomach wound was no small matter, and Brant wanted someone watching the boy all the time so that they could catch any infections early on.

When Brant walked in, Matthew was sleeping and James stood over a table, quietly looking over some of the doctor's tools.

"And what might you be doing?"

James spun around to face his brother, dropping a scalpel in the process, guilt written on his face. "Nothing."

"You shouldn't be snooping."

"I was just looking."

Brant smiled. "I won't tell the doc, but you better be careful. He's likely to carve you up if he catches you playing with his instruments," he joked, which was received with wide eyes of fear from James.

"You can go. I'll watch him until the doctor takes over for the night."

"Do I have to do this again tomorrow?"

"Yes, and every other day until he is strong enough to be out of danger."

James groaned but nodded his assent—not daring to complain.

"I'll have someone else do latrine duty. Would that make up for this?"

"I'd watch every patient if it meant I never had to carry another latrine pail again!"

Brant laughed. "Well, I hope we don't have patients that often. Now go have some dinner. Cook is just about to serve the men."

James ran off at the mention of food and left him alone with the sleeping boy. Brant sat down and sighed. He didn't know what was going to happen to the boy, but he was too young to be walking the thin line between life and death. It was a scary thought, but that could have been him if Captain LaFleur had allowed him to fight before he was ready. And it could be James if Brant ever lost track of what was important. He could never live with himself if James had to pay for his life choices.

Matthew stirred slightly, and then opened his eyes, looking at Brant through heavily lidded eyes. "Hello."

Brant smiled. "Hello, Matthew. How're you doing today?"

"Okay, I suppose. Where's James?"

"I sent him to get some dinner. The doctor will be bringing you some food shortly. Are you hungry?"

As if in reply Matthew's stomach growled loudly and he looked up at Brant sheepishly. "A little."

"If you don't mind me asking, is it normal for a boy of your age to help defend the ship?"

He nodded. "I ain't part of the navy but I serve on a British ship; we are all expected to come to the aid of our ship."

"Are you in much pain?"

"Hurts a bit, yeah. Doc says he ain't got much for the pain, so I mostly try to sleep so that I can forget about it. I'm afraid I'm not very good company for James."

"That's fine. James is here for you and he is getting out of a lot of work to sit here. What do you plan on doing after you're healed?"

"I dunno. You say you dock in London in a couple months?"

"Yes. Would you like to get off there?"

"I ain't got anyone left in England. My mum and dad died a couple years ago so I joined a crew for three square meals a day. I suppose I'll try to sign onto another ship."

Brant nodded. "Well you're more than welcome to continue your training here. Casper doesn't have a sailing mate as of yet."

"Thank you, Captain."

"It's just an option for you. You don't owe us anything."

Matthew nodded, but looked over towards the door as the doctor walked in. "Guess I gotta work hard at getting better first."

Brant nodded. "Hello, Doc. I'll leave you to your patient."

He left the cramped room and went to have his dinner in the dining room with the infuriating Catherine Marshall. If only she would just keep her snobbish little nose in her cabin and leave him alone for the next two months; then life would be good.

* * *

Catherine paced back and forth in her cabin. She hadn't emerged from it since earlier that afternoon, and she was still nursing a bruised ego. She contemplated skipping dinner and staying in her cabin, but she was much too hungry not to eat, and she wasn't so confident Captain Foxton would send a tray to her room. So, she swallowed her pride and stepped out of her cabin and into the dining room next door. The cook was just setting out the food, similar to what they had the night before; fruit, salted meat and potatoes. Catherine was sick of this food already and desperately hoped that she wouldn't have to live off of it for the entire voyage home—there was only so much salted pork one could eat.

The captain stood as she entered and once again pulled out her chair, but this time he sat her further away, on the opposite side of the table from him next to a young man named Casper, not that she really cared.

It was apparent that the captain didn't really wish to speak with her after their falling out that afternoon and she couldn't help but feel a little thankful for that—she wasn't really in the right frame of mind to talk to him either. But, he was intriguing, she had to admit.

Karl was the one that carried the conversation that evening, attempting to draw both Catherine and Brant into discussion, but both only answered briefly and tersely any questions or comments directed at them.

Catherine didn't much care for Karl. He was middle aged and quite obviously lower class, but the captain seemed to look up to him and value his opinion. But why, she didn't know. He was obviously an uneducated man. How much wisdom could he truly offer?

As soon as Catherine could politely excuse herself she did, and returned to her cabin where she locked herself in and went to bed.

* * *

Brant was restless. There was nothing to do but sail, sail, and sail some more. No raids, little to no repairs, and calm waters. Brant was almost hoping for a storm to add some excitement and extra work into their lives—anything to chase the boredom away.

Catherine still rarely emerged from her cabin except for dinner—a torturous and unpleasant affair. They hadn't exchanged more than a dozen words since their original argument over a week earlier, and Brant wasn't about to be the first person to apologize. He was giving the woman passage, and if she wanted to make things right, she could. Otherwise, she was just a job for him.

James sat daily with Matthew, and Brant saw the boy continually improving. He was a fighter that was for certain. The wound had not yet fully closed and there was still a danger of infection, but that danger was becoming less and less likely with every passing day. Matthew seemed to be sleeping a lot less and was getting along well with James, who was teaching him how to read since he only knew a few basic things that he was required to know to read a map. It was nice to see James with someone close to his own age, coming out of his shell. Brant was seeing a side of James he didn't get to see often; how he interacted with peers.

"Brant!" James came running up from below deck to where Brant was sitting with Joseph repairing an old sail.

Brant dropped the sail and jumped up from where he had been sitting. "Something happen with Matthew?"

James nodded, eyes wide with fear. "Something is wrong. He was just sleeping and he started rolling around groaning, and he is sweating and burning to touch."

"Go get the doc. He's in the galley," commanded Brant, already walking towards the doctor's cabin that doubled as an infirmary. Bursting into the room he was greeted by the sight of Matthew drenched in sweat and pale as death. Brant drew back his blanket and gingerly began unwrapping the bandage. He winced at the pungent smell that rose from what looked to be a festering wound. Things had taken a turn for the worse quickly and with no warning.

The doctor burst into the room seconds later, red in the face from what must have been a sprint from the galley, and pushed Brant aside. Looking at the wound he shook his head. "It's not good, Captain. I can clean it, but we have to let it drain and the infection has to heal before I can let the wound close."

"He was doing so well."

"Stomach wounds are incredibly volatile. I thought an infection would have set in long ago," he paused, then frowned. "James, you need to leave."

Brant turned to see his brother standing in the doorway looking at his friend in horror.

"Is he going to die?"

Brant looked at his brother in sorrow. He was only eleven. He shouldn't be considering the fact that a young man—no, boy—was going to die. "Not if the doctor can help it. Now go."

James left the room, and Brant turned back to the doctor. "What can I do?"

"Go boil me some water, quick. This wound needs to be reopened to properly drain."

Brant rushed off to the galley, and quickly set a pot of water over a blazing fire, but every second waiting for the water to boil seemed like a second too long.

As the water began to boil Brant grabbed a rag, wrapping it around the piping hot handle, and nearly ran with it back to the doctor.

"Put it over there." He pointed absently as he set out his tools. He threw a couple scalpels in the water and with tongs pulled them out, wiped them off and then got a clean rag to clean the wound.

"Get me my leather stick."

Brant looked through his cupboards and found it, handing it over. The doctor pried open Matthew's jaw and placed it between his teeth. "This is going to hurt. I need you to hold him down."

Brant nodded and put his hands on the boy's shoulders. Doc lifted his scalpel and inserted it into the infected wound, slowly drawing it across the tender flesh, reopening it to the elements. Matthew's eyes flew open and he ground his teeth into the leather while struggling to get free.

"Easy, Matthew. It has to be done or you'll die." That didn't seem to settle the boy down, and Brant held him down firmly while the doc grabbed some alcohol and poured it over the injury. As the liquid hit the tender, raw flesh, Matthew screamed and bucked against Brant's strong arms.

With the wound cleaned, the doctor redressed it and went to clean his tools. Matthew lay there sobbing in pain. Letting go, Brant gently patted his shoulder. "It's over. It's okay."

"The wound will have to drain for the next couple of days but as soon as the infection looks like it has passed I'll stitch him up."

Brant nodded. "If you need any help James is at your disposal. And please, let me know of any changes."

The doctor nodded and Brant took his leave, unable to handle the stench of rotting flesh mixed with sweat.

* * *

Brant didn't attend dinner that evening—he had lost his appetite after the events with Matthew, and had no energy to deal with *Lady* Catherine Marshall. Instead he climbed up to the crow's nest and sat there for most of the evening, watching the small amount of activity below him as a card game went on in one corner and a couple men played various instruments near the mast. Catherine caught Brant's attention as she practically floated over the deck towards the dining room, but he had no wish to speak to her. He knew that at some point he would have to break their silence before the voyage was over, but for now it was just easier to avoid her. Right now his first concern was Matthew. The petty concerns of a spoiled rich girl were trivial and unimportant at the moment.

For five days he skipped dinner, taking a small amount of food from the kitchen and eating it alone up in the crow's nest. Karl, for once, didn't interfere with Brant's self-imposed exile. Matthew's infection raged on and he was becoming weaker and weaker with each passing day. Brant begged the doctor to do something, anything to get him better but he would only shake his head and say they were already doing everything they could. The alcohol was killing everything, bacteria good and bad, and yet the infection raged on. "What about heat?" Brant asked one day. "Could we not kill the infection off for good with heat? Cauterize the wound?"

The doctor nodded. "We could, but I'm worried the infection will get locked inside then. Cauterizing is best done before infection sets in."

"So we have to continue to allow the wound to drain and hope that one day the infection will die?"

"It's largely up to Matthew now. His body has to do most of the fighting. We're keeping it as clean as we can."

"He isn't strong enough to do that anymore. He's weaker every day."

"I don't think he'll make it. I'm sorry, Captain."

Brant shook his head. "He'll make it. You are going to do everything you can. Try something new and get that infection killed. He's going to make it."

"It'll be nothing short of a miracle if he survives this."

"Miracles happen every day. Make me a miracle, Doctor."

The doctor threw up his hands in frustration as Brant walked out. Never before had Brant asked the impossible of anyone in his crew. He always expected their best work, but never the impossible. But he couldn't have the boy die on his ship. He couldn't accept that there was nothing left, that someone so young would leave this world because of the cruelty of man.

* * *

Catherine knew little of what was occurring around the ship since her boredom had yet to force her out of her cabin at any time other than dinner. The captain's absence at dinner the past few days did not go unnoticed, and was a welcome relief from the usually tense meals they shared. But, after a week of obvious avoidance, Catherine was beginning to feel like his absence was a personal affront. And, as much as she hated to admit it, she was beginning to feel lonely. So, gathering her pride she left the safe confines of her cabin and found the quarter master, Karl.

"What is wrong with the captain?"

"What do you mean?"

"He hasn't been to dinner in over a week. Have I done something to upset him?"

"Nay, tis nothing to do with you, ma'am. The captain be a bit on the low side because that boy they rescued off your ship be on death's doorstep. Doc says there ain't nothin' he can do anymore and that boy be too weak to fight off infection on his own."

Catherine nodded soberly, but inside she was churning. She hadn't even afforded the boy a second thought since their rescue. Everything had been about her, about wearing stolen clothes, eating bad food, and eating dinner in the company of sailors. She hadn't once stopped to wonder about the welfare of the boy, and here he was dying while she complained of trivial things. "Can I see the boy?"

Karl nodded. "Not much can make things worse now. Come with me."

Karl led Catherine to the small room where she stood looking at the boy. He was pale, sweaty, and breathing heavily. A lump grew in her throat as she tried to swallow down the tears that welled up. He was too young to die. He had barely lived—had so many years ahead of him. "Please bring me some clean water and a cloth," she instructed as she sat down on the small stool next to the boy. Karl nodded and left to get what she had requested.

Catherine reached out and gently brushed the boy's hair away from his face. Drawing back the blanket, she gingerly removed the bandage. The wound was inflamed and oozing and it smelled a bit of rotting flesh. Karl returned with the water and she gently cleaned the boy's face of sweat. "What is his name?"

"Matthew."

"Can you get the doctor for me?"

Karl trotted off and came back moments later with the doctor.

"Can I help you?"

"What have you been cleaning the wound with?"

"Alcohol."

"Let's try salt water."

"What?" The doctor looked thoroughly confused.

"When my father was in Spain one summer, someone had tried to kill him. His wound became infected and the doctor there cleaned it with salt water."

The doctor nodded thoughtfully. "Well it can't cause any harm, I suppose. The boy is already going to die if something drastic doesn't happen. I'll go boil a pot."

Catherine held the boy's hand until the doctor came back. As they waited for the water to cool off a bit, Catherine continued to clean off his face. "If this doesn't work how long do you think he'll have?"

"It's hard to say. Maybe a day or two, maybe a week."

The doctor handed Catherine a cup full of salt water and a rag and she took it nervously. She had never treated anyone with a wound before. She had only ever seen her father being taken care of, and now she was to do the job of a common nurse. Taking the rag she dipped it in the water and gently dabbed it on the wound, cleaning away the oozing liquid. Matthew began to moan but he was too weak to fight.

"The doctor never dressed my father's wounds. He said fresh air was the best thing for infection."

"Very well. I'll watch him to make sure he doesn't touch anything then. We'll try this treatment for a little while and see if it shows any improvement."

Catherine nodded and exited the cabin. She needed to get out of the stuffy room and into fresh air. Taking deep breaths, she looked up at the crow's nest and wondered if the captain was up there. She couldn't see anything from her location, so she went back into her cabin and locked the door—once again successfully cutting herself off from a world that she wanted nothing to do with. Sitting down on a chair by the window that looked out the rear of the ship towards the open ocean, Catherine pulled out a book and read until dinner time.

* * *

Brant went down to check on Matthew later that day and was surprised to see that there was no dressing on his wound. "Why did you do this?" he asked, pointing at the wound open to the air.

"Lady Marshall and I are trying a new approach."

"Lady Marshall?"

"Yes. She came by today and suggested a treatment that she had seen used successfully in Spain."

"I see. And is it working?"

"It's too soon to say but we'll give it a couple days to prove itself."

"And then?"

"And if it's not working the boy will die. He's been largely unconscious or incoherent for over a week, Captain. He's on his last legs."

Brant nodded. "I'll be back tomorrow."

He was there every day checking in on Matthew and watching him improve. The saltwater was making a difference, and although the doctor was happy with his improvements, he still gave no promises that the boy would make it.

Brant avoided visiting at the same time as Catherine, but he noticed her every day as she made the short walk to the doctor's quarters below deck. Brant knew he should thank her for what she had done to help Matthew, even after she had made it very clear she wanted nothing to do with anyone on the ship, but his pride held him back. She had insulted him, his men, and his profession. She had shown him one side of her and he had readily accepted it as all there was to Catherine Marshall, but now he was seeing something completely different. Who was she and was she the spoiled rich girl he'd first met, or this kind and caring woman nursing a boy back to health?

* * *

Catherine walked into the doctor's quarters two weeks after the saltwater treatments had begun and greeted Matthew, who was now awake, sitting up, and more energetic than he had been since he had arrived on the ship.

"Good morning, Matthew. How're you doing today?"

"Great. Look, it's starting to close up!" Matthew lifted his shirt to show off the scabbing wound. It looked like a healthy, healing wound, and it couldn't have made Catherine happier.

"That's wonderful! Before you know it you'll be running around the deck causing all kinds of trouble."

He smiled and lowered his shirt again. "The doctor says I still have to take it easy even though I'm feeling great."

"Doctor knows best."

He grumbled a little which brought a laugh out of Catherine. She spent the entire morning with him, talking and reading to him. James came in the afternoon and they continued with their reading lessons that they had begun before the infection had set in.

Brant had stopped visiting every day since it became apparent that Matthew would survive, and he went back to going about his normal duties. He stopped hiding up in the crow's nest and even ate dinner with Catherine on occasion, but he still refused to talk to her, and it was beginning to frustrate her.

When she left Matthew later that day she went in search of Brant and found him talking with Casper over a map.

"May I speak with you?" she asked.

Brant looked up, annoyance written all over his face. "Give me a moment. I'm busy."

"Fine. I'll wait." Catherine walked over to the railing directly behind Brant and Casper and paced back and forth until Brant came over about twenty minutes later.

"What would you like, your highness?" he asked, mocking condescension dripping from his words.

"First of all, I would appreciate at least some semblance of respect. My name is Catherine Marshall. If you can't say miss or lady then at least just call me Catherine."

"Are you dropping decorum?"

"I'm afraid it's nearly useless out here, Captain."

"And what was it that you wanted, Catherine?" He spoke gentler this time.

"I want to break this silence of ours. We had an argument and it has made life on this ship very difficult and awkward. Can we at least try and get along for the remainder of the voyage?"

"Of course, but you have to be less demeaning to my men. On my ship there is no social class, just human beings."

"I will do my best."

"And you don't wish us dead anymore?"

Catherine laughed. "Oh, I still think you're a bunch of common criminals who deserve to be hung, but I'll try not to voice that sentiment."

Brant smiled. "I can live with that. I'm pretty sure even the king harbors those feelings. And please, call me Brant."

"Does that mean you will be having dinner with me tonight, Brant?"

"It does."

Catherine smiled and walked away, leaving him to do his work. She hadn't expected that conversation to go so well. In fact, she had half expected it to blow up in her face and turn into another argument. Instead she had been pleasantly surprised by Brant's civility. He had struck her as more of a hot head when they had first met, but then again he confused her more and more each day. One minute he was a gentleman, the next a rogue, the next brooding and then suddenly he was friendly. He had too many faces to put a finger on his personality.

Dinner was an interesting affair that night. Brant seated her next to him for the first time in over three weeks, and he spoke with her, joked, and even teased her a little. She tried to carry on conversations with the other officers. She had already spoken with Karl on numerous occasions, but it was hard to forget her upbringing. She kept telling herself that it was okay to talk to these men and that no one would frown on her behavior, but it was hard to let go of rules that had been ingrained in her since childhood.

After dinner Brant walked with Catherine back to her cabin. As he opened the door for her she turned to him and stopped. "Will you be climbing up to the crow's nest now?"

Brant looked at her questioningly and nodded. "Yes."

"Why do you go up there?"

"To think. It's the most isolated place I know, and the view is spectacular. Would you like to come?"

Catherine shook her head. "Maybe some other time. Good night, Captain."

"Goodnight, Catherine."

Brant walked away leaving Catherine alone in the doorway of her cabin.

CHAPTER ELEVEN

Brant found himself enjoying Catherine's company now that they had agreed to be civil and attempt a friendship. Quite often he found himself getting caught up in conversation with her throughout the day. She had many questions about the ship and how things were run, which Brant was more than happy to answer. He was beginning to regret ever thinking she was uneducated or naïve; it seemed like she wanted to learn everything she could about her surroundings and he was quickly beginning to realize through their conversations that she knew quite a bit about politics and the state of the current world.

That evening, after dinner Catherine joined Brant on a walk around the deck.

"I won't deny the usefulness of the economic warfare privateers wage on the Spanish. But, don't you think that eventually they'll get tired of it and rise up? They're prideful people and won't sit idly by forever, nor will they accept the excuse that men like you are acting of your own volition outside of the law."

Brant nodded "But you can't deny that if we weren't making their country poorer, then they probably would have already declared war."

"Possibly, but if the pot wasn't being continually stirred, a more stable peace may have been negotiated by now. The Spanish are becoming extremely angry and it's becoming more and more dangerous for my father to make his trips there. Pretty soon he will be unable to safely go there, and then we will be on the brink of war. Spain still thinks that England is rightfully theirs after Prince Philip married Bloody Mary."

"Then how will negotiations change their mind?"

"It would buy us some time."

"See, now you're going back on what you said. We're buying you time already, and making England richer in the process."

"Do you want me to say you are serving your country?"

"That would be nice."

"Well, I won't, Brant Foxton. You can dress up a pig, but a pig is still a pig. We can give you a letter making you untouchable, but you're still a murderer and thief."

Brant smirked. "A pig, huh? And do you still have a problem with that, with me?"

Catherine smiled slightly and turned to face him. "When it comes to you, my convictions are beginning to crumble a bit. But overall, my view of privateering remains the same."

"Good. Then I suppose your time here will not be such a waste after all."

Catherine laughed and continued walking the perimeter of the ship. "Depends what you consider a waste."

He smiled and fell back into step beside her. They completed their round, and he walked her back to her cabin where he wished her good night and went to climb up to the crow's nest to clear his head for the day. However, this evening his mind was full of the sophisticated young woman who had taken up residence in his cabin. He found himself enjoying her company more and more, and was already looking forward to when morning would dawn and he could see her again.

* * *

Brant was disappointed that Catherine spent most of the next morning with Matthew, rather than him, but he was glad to see how caring and kind she was being. It was like he was seeing a whole different woman than the one that had been held back by class just a few short weeks ago.

So, taking advantage of Catherine being busy, he holed himself up in his cabin that he had been letting her use, and looked over some paperwork. James had taken inventory last week and supplies were getting low, but there weren't many places to stop any more. Studying the map, Brant decided that they would make port in Casablanca, Morocco and pick up supplies, spend a few days for some much needed rest, and then continue on their way. Brant hoped that they would reach their destination in another month after that.

Calling Casper in, Brant went over the detour in their course and sent him to make the appropriate changes. He was so busy with paperwork and inventory lists that he didn't even notice Catherine walk in.

"I see you're making use of your desk."

Brant looked up and smiled. "I'm afraid I couldn't put my paperwork off any longer. I'm sorry if I invaded your space."

"Not at all. It's fine."

"You sure do leave it messy though," Brant said, frowning as he looked around the room at the various items of clothing strewn around the floor.

"Normally I would be travelling with my hand maiden but she was taken during the attack."

Brant studied Catherine's face, searching for any sign of sorrow or sadness for the fate of the girl who had spent so much time with her. "Aren't you upset about that?"

"Well, yes, but at least she isn't dead."

"She might as well be."

Catherine was taken aback. "What did they do to her?"

"Likely sold her into slavery. Old Richard is not a kind man and he'll make a profit off of whatever he can."

Catherine paled but held herself strong. "I wish you didn't tell me that."

He shrugged. "You should be more aware of some of the evils in the world."

She nodded and walked over to the chair she had placed next to the large rear facing window and sat down, picking up her book and reading. Brant watched her for a few minutes and then went back to the work at hand.

"I'm sorry," he said after a time.

Catherine looked up. "It's okay."

"I shouldn't have told you that."

"It's okay. You're right; I need to be more aware."

They fell back into their silence, one reading, the other working until

James came to tell them dinner was ready.

Both putting down what had been occupying their attention for the last few hours, Brant and Catherine walked together to the dining room. It was a pleasant dinner. Most of them had been since Brant and Catherine had stopped their feuding, but this one seemed to have a particular joy about it. There was more laughter than usual, and everyone seemed to be in good spirits. Perhaps because it had been weeks since any of them had to kill a man or commit a crime… Or perhaps it was just something in the air. Whatever it was, Brant liked it.

After dinner, when he walked Catherine back to her cabin, he invited her to join him up on the crow's nest.

"Oh, I couldn't! It's so very high and dresses are not meant for climbing in."

He laughed. "Then change. Borrow a pair of my breeches."

She looked thoughtful but laughed and shook her head in protest again. "I can't!"

"You can do anything you put your mind to, Miss Marshall."

"Not this."

"Anything."

Catherine threw up her hands in surrender. "Fine! Just let me change."

She disappeared into the cabin and came back out moments later in a pair of Brant's breeches that fit her quite nicely, clinging closely in all the right places. "Okay, let's go before I change my mind."

Brant laughed and took her hand, leading her towards the mast and the long climb up to the lookout post, otherwise known as the crow's nest.

"You go up first. I'll be right behind you to make sure you don't fall."

"Now I'm really glad I'm not wearing a dress," she mumbled as she began climbing. Brant chuckled and followed a few rungs behind.

"You think that I'd be so dishonorable as to peek up a ladies dress?"

"I wouldn't put anything past you, Captain Brant Foxton."

He laughed loudly and fully. "You make me out to be such a rogue!"

Catherine mumbled something under her breath that he didn't manage to catch, but he figured it wasn't very nice anyway, so it probably wasn't worth hearing.

As they climbed the last few rungs, Catherine pulled herself up onto the platform, Brant right behind. She was panting slightly from the exertion, not used to physical activity, but she was smiling wildly as she looked around. "This is amazing, Brant."

"You're glad you made the climb?"

"Yes, very much so. Thank you."

Brant smiled and put his arm around her—telling himself it was to protect her from the cool breeze, but really he just enjoyed the feeling of her in his arms.

"I can understand why you come up here so often. It's incredibly peaceful."

"It is, so don't you go invading my personal time now. Even captains need to clear their heads sometimes."

Catherine smiled and snuggled in a little closer as a burst of cold wind enveloped them.

"It won't be long now until we reach London, you know."

Catherine nodded. "Yes. I'm looking forward to being home again. How long have we been sailing?"

"Just over a month. We're going to make port in Casablanca, Morocco for a couple of days. If you like I can take you to shore so that you can explore a bit."

"Could you? I think I would enjoy that."

They fell into a comfortable silence for a while—both alone in their thoughts. It was quite unbelievable to Brant that he had such a beautiful and smart woman sitting with him in the crow's nest of his own ship. He almost dreaded the day that they would dock in London and she would walk out of his life for good.

"Are you happy here, Catherine?" he asked, breaking the silence.

She didn't answer right away, mulling his question over for a couple of minutes. "I suppose I am. I've never been able to let go of my inhibitions quite like I've been able to here. And it's very refreshing to have you, a man, see me as an intelligent person. In my circles women are expected to be good at running their house and raising a family, which is all very good, but sometimes I wish the men would talk politics with me. My father is the only man who ever has before you. It's refreshing. Thank you, Brant."

"You're a very smart woman, Catherine. You should let people know. What's stopping you from joining in the men's conversations if that is what you wish to discuss?"

"Decorum."

Brant nodded. "Of course. You know, you and I didn't start out so differently."

Catherine turned to face Brant, moving out from under his arm in the process. "Am I going to hear the story of Brant Foxton's past?"

"If you care to sit through it. It's a long one."

"Please."

Brant sighed and looked out to the ocean. "Not tonight. It's getting late. I promise I will tell you soon, though."

Catherine looked disappointed, but she forced a smile and stood up, allowing Brant to lead the way down the ladder.

* * *

Catherine didn't see much of Brant the next couple days as they drew closer to land and made their way up the coastline to Morocco. She found herself missing his company but she kept herself busy by looking after Matthew and reading. She would watch the crew from time-to-time, wondering about their lives outside of the *BlackFox*. Did they have families or sweethearts they had left behind?

Eventually it grew tiring, so she retreated to her cabin where she spent the remainder of the afternoon reading. Brant had a good sized collection of books, and Catherine was enjoying it immensely. She had finished multiple books, being as there wasn't much of anything else for her to fill her time with. After dinner she finally got Brant to herself again, the first time in three days.

"You've been busy lately."

Brant strolled with her around the deck. "Yes. Casper isn't quite what a sailing master should be, so when it comes to navigating closer to shore I have to step in. It will be like this for most of the remaining voyage."

"So I shall have no friend to talk to?"

Brant smiled. "I'll still make time for you. Don't you worry about that."

"And you still have to tell me your story. You promised."

"Be patient. I will tell you in good time. Don't forget that it won't be long before we dock in Casablanca and then we can explore the beauties of Morocco for a few days. I'm giving you one thing to look forward to at a time."

"So you're saying that I won't hear the story until after Casablanca?"

"Correct."

Catherine pouted a little, causing Brant to laugh. "You're much prettier when you smile. Don't look so disappointed, it will be worth the wait."

"It had better be."

"And if it isn't?"

"Then I won't be your friend anymore. I cannot abide a liar."

Brant laughed and opened the door to Catherine's cabin. "I'm going to have to bid you good night now. I'm afraid I have an early start in the morning as we expect to be getting close to land."

"Good night, Brant." She kissed him on the cheek before ducking into her cabin and closing the door behind her, but not before seeing the shocked look and blush creeping up Brant's face as he stood, stock still and dumbfounded.

* * *

When they docked in Casablanca on Friday, Brant went in search of Catherine to bring her ashore, as promised. But, she was nowhere to be found. He went around to the crew members asking if they had seen her, but they all shook their heads. How a young woman had just disappeared off a ship was beyond him. Not sure where she was, he decided to leave for the afternoon, hoping that she would show up for dinner. Walking down the ramp, he heard a woman shouting his name. Looking around, he saw no one, but then he looked up and saw Catherine standing in the crow's nest waving down at him. She had a pair of his breeches on again, and her long blonde hair, which was usually done up carefully, was flowing freely in the wind like a banner. Chuckling, he trotted back up on deck and climbed up to meet her.

"What are you doing up here? I've been looking everywhere."

"I wanted to see the city as we sailed into the harbor, and what better vantage point than the crow's nest?"

Brant shook his head laughed. "Would you like to actually go into the city now?"

"Oh yes! Just let me get changed into something more proper."

Brant shook his head. "Either you come right this minute or you have to wait till tomorrow." He wasn't willing to wait for her to get laced and buttoned in to a dress just so that she could look the part of a lady.

Catherine frowned. "But I can't be seen dressed like this."

"I'm seeing you right now."

"And if I wait till tomorrow?"

Brant shrugged.

"Fine then, but I'll have you know that I think this is highly inappropriate."

"You're sailing on a privateer ship. There has been nothing appropriate about your life for the last month."

She smiled slightly and climbed down the ladder, more confident now than she had been last week when Brant had brought her up.

Walking through the streets of Casablanca, they were bombarded with many colors and loud noises. There were street vendors everywhere. Everyone wanted them to buy their goods or food. There were skinny children that held out their bowls to beg, but some guards chased them away.

"Did you want to buy anything?" Brant asked as he caught Catherine looking at a table full of fabric.

"All my money was stolen during the raid."

Brant walked over to join her at the table and turned some of the fabric over in his hand. "Which one do you like?"

Catherine pointed at a bright blue bolt of fabric inlaid with silver designs. Brant picked it up, turned it over a couple of times and ran some fabric through his fingers. Nodding slightly he turned to the woman watching the table. "How much?"

"Fifty Durham."

Brant whistled but nodded. "I have here," he counted out thirty pieces of eight, "thirty Spanish Reals. Good?"

Catherine shook her head, grabbing Brant's arm. "It's too much, Brant. What will I do with it?"

"And I will need some needles and thread."

The shopkeeper nodded her head fervently and held out her hands greedily. The Spanish Real was worth nearly double the Moroccan Durham. Brant shook his head. "No, you wrap up that fabric first with needles and thread. Then I pay you."

The woman shrugged and pulled out some brown paper which she wrapped the bolt of fabric in then she pulled out some spools of blue thread and two needles which she added to the package. Holding out her hand again, Brant dumped the money in her hand and took the package. Handing it over to Catherine, he smiled. "There you are. Something to keep you occupied for a few days."

"Really, it is too much."

"Nonsense! You deserve the best."

"I will pay you back once we reach England."

"You will do no such thing," he said firmly. "This is a gift."

Catherine gave up and nodded. "Thank you, Brant."

"See, that's all I wanted to hear. You're most welcome, Catherine. Now come along, there is still much to see."

* * *

They stayed in Casablanca for a week, allowing the crew of the *BlackFox* a short leave while Brant looked after supplying the ship. On the morning they were to leave, the crew was busy loading supplies that had been delivered the night before. Catherine climbed up to the crow's nest again, where she was out of the way and could watch the departure. She had become comfortable with climbing up there and found herself enjoying the view more than she had the first time. She could see the expanse of the entire city; there were houses everywhere and people milling about the streets. It was a truly amazing city that Catherine was sure she never would have been able to experience under normal circumstances. She was almost sad to leave, but casting off meant that they were bringing her home and she desperately missed it. By now some kind of report had probably made it back to her parents that her ship had been attacked. Would they think she was dead, or would they be holding on to hope that she had found rescue?

As the *BlackFox* cast off around mid-morning, Catherine stood up. Holding the mast tightly for support, she watched the city slowly disappear on the horizon. Her journey was nearly done now, only the last leg left. She stayed up there until Casablanca was out of sight and then climbed down to look in on Matthew, whom she hadn't seen much of in the last week. As her feet touched the deck she heard her name being called. Looking in the direction of the hold, she saw Matthew standing there, smiling broadly. "Catherine, look! The doc said I could get up now."

She walked over and hugged him. "That's wonderful! But you still have to be gentle. No running around or hard work, your wound is still tender."

"I'm just happy to be out of that stuffy room. The doc said we were in Casablanca, but he wouldn't let me get out of bed and see. Was it amazing?"

Catherine laughed. "It was. Come, walk with me. A little exercise will do you good."

Matthew walked with her and she told him all about the sights she had seen in the colorful city. He listened, wide eyed and excited, exclaiming over some of the stories. After an hour of walking Catherine made Matthew sit down and rest. He insisted he was still feeling well, but he had grown pale and she could tell he was fatigued. He wasn't ready to exert himself so much, not after being so close to death. Sending him off to his bed for a rest, she shushed all his attempts at protest and closed the door behind her. Walking back on deck she was greeted by Brant standing there with his hands crossed.

"Well, aren't you the mother hen?"

Catherine laughed. "The boy needs looking after. You men just never know when to stop."

Brant nodded his assent and offered her his arm. "Come, have lunch with me."

"Lunch?" Catherine had learned quickly that there was no formal lunch, and after a week of starving she had made her way to the galley to beg food from the cook.

"Yes, lunch. We have a boatload of fresh fruit, vegetables, and meat, the unsalted kind, which need eating before it all goes bad."

"Real meat?"

Brant laughed. "Yes ma'am. But not much, so we had best go eat some for lunch now before it's all gone."

Catherine's stomach grumbled slightly and she laughed. "Lead the way. I think my stomach is about to eat itself."

"We can't have that, now can we?"

Brant led her down to the galley where most of the crew had gathered.

He seated her at a table with James, Casper and a few of the younger sailors.

She turned to Brant and whispered "What is all this about? We're eating with the crew?" Catherine thought that she was doing well, treating the men with respect and kindness, but this was too much. She wasn't sure she could eat with these men, the crude joking and interesting mixture of smells meeting her nose.

Brant gave her a disappointed look. "Yes, we're eating with the crew. It's something I do with the men when we leave a port and have fresh stock. They all get to eat the fresh food, and the officers and I join them."

Determined not to disappoint Brant, she smiled graciously and didn't protest. She made an effort to speak with the men as best she could, but their raucous laughter and crude conversations left her mostly appalled and uncomfortable. However, she spoke no word of complaint, and hoped that she wouldn't have to endure such a meal again, nor would she ever admit to having this one. Brant had pushed her too far, but it would have to wait until later to be dealt with.

* * *

Later that night, Brant climbed up to the crow's nest. It didn't take long for Catherine to appear, climbing onto the platform and sitting next to him.

"I need to talk to you."

Brant nodded, as if he had been expecting this conversation.

"This afternoon, at lunch, I found it to be a very uncomfortable situation. I'm not trying to be pretentious or snobbish, but the men in the crew can be very crude and a lot of conversation during lunch was offensive and embarrassing for me. I have nothing against the crew, I just found it inappropriate that I would join them for lunch in the galley."

Brant nodded slightly and put his arm around her. "I understand. I shouldn't have pushed you. You've had to overcome a lot, and you've grown as a person. I don't think you're being pretentious; the galley is no place for a woman of any standing, and I should have realized that."

They sat in silence for a time, and Catherine rested her head on Brant's strong shoulder. "Can I hear your story now?"

"Is that what you want?"

"Mmmhmm."

"Alright. I was born to Sir Calvin and Suzanne Foxton, you may recognize the name…"

Brant told her of how his mother died, how he left home to follow his dreams of being a captain and stumbled into the situation of joining a privateering ship. How he had found it immoral and hard to swallow at first. He told her of the years of training in swordsmanship, and the tests LaFleur had him perform. He told her of the mutiny and LaFleur's death, and his ultimate rise to captaincy. Then, the death of his father, Calvin Foxton and the guardianship of James. There was a lot to tell, and they sat up in the crow's nest for two hours as Brant narrated his life so far. Catherine listened in wonder as she tried to fathom him leaving a life where everything was set, for an unsure future.

"I never knew," she whispered softly as his story drew to a close. "You've been through so much and made a lot of hard decisions. I have to admit, I admire you for what you have done."

"You can admire a murderer and criminal?"

"Not that, but you as a person, I can. I could never leave my life for something like this."

"My father still ensured that my future was secure before he died. I own his sugar plantation in Jamaica."

"Yes, but you had no idea you'd be receiving that. You left thinking that you would be on your own from that point on, and likely never to see your family again. It's admirable. Foolhardy, but admirable."

Brant laughed and squeezed her closer to his side. It was probably inappropriate, how close they sat when they were up here, but there was no one to witness and neither seemed to care.

"You are an amazing woman, Catherine. I don't want you to ever forget that."

"Thank you."

Brant kissed the top of her head and stroked her hair gently as her head rested on his shoulder. A few moments later he felt the steady breathing of sleep take over her and he smiled. He would be unable to carry her down, and he couldn't find it in his heart to wake her, so he put both arms around her and settled in for a long night.

CHAPTER TWELVE

Brant was woken up by a bright, warm light shining down on him. It took a minute to remember where he was, but as he opened his eyes and the morning breeze caressed his senses back to life, he remembered the night before. He was high above the deck of the ship in the crow's nest with a very beautiful woman sleeping in his arms. Smiling, Brant gently shook her awake. Catherine groaned and opened her eyes a little.

"Where are we?"

"I'm afraid we spent the night in the crow's nest."

"What?" Catherine sleepily looked around and sighed. "I fell asleep didn't I? Why didn't you wake me?"

"I didn't want to disturb you. Don't worry about it; this is the best I've slept in a while."

And, as if on cue, Brant's stomach rumbled. "But, I need breakfast. Come on, let's go down and get some food in you."

Catherine stretched a little and climbed down behind Brant. It was still early, the sun having woken them at the break of dawn, and most of the crew were still in their bunks. Only a small skeleton crew of men wandered the deck going about the small daily jobs that were needed to keep the ship sailing smoothly. Brant said good morning to most as he walked by and led Catherine to her cabin.

"You freshen up. I will go rustle up some breakfast and bring it here."

In the kitchen he found some fresh baked bread and fried up some meat and eggs. With breakfast ready to go, he filled up two plates and took them back to Catherine's cabin.

"Here we are, fresh served off the grill." He handed her a plate and she took the chair at his desk while Brant sat on the floor, leaning against the wall.

Catherine took a few bites and nodded her approval. "I didn't know you could cook."

"Not very well. As a cabin boy I was on breakfast duty for a while with the cook. Most of the time we just made mush he called porridge, but every once in a while we would have fresh eggs."

"I'm very impressed. I couldn't do this."

Brant laughed. "That's because you have maids to do it for you."

Catherine nodded her assent and continued to eat the meal. After finishing she turned to face Brant, a frown marring her face.

"What?"

"Nothing. It's just... strange."

"What is?"

"This relationship we have. I'm normally a very reserved person but you make me... not reserved."

"Is that a bad thing?"

"I'm not entirely sure. I liked the old me. It worked well."

"And how is this working for you?"

"It's different. Not good or bad, just different."

"I see." Brant got up from the floor and walked over to her, cupping her face in his hands. He studied her face and her wide, innocent eyes and found himself enraptured. She was a famed siren of the sea, there was no other explanation for the strange and unexplainable allure she had. "I think you are a beautiful and intelligent woman who needs to let that shine, Catherine. You hide too much."

Her eyes were locked on his and he couldn't look away. She said nothing, and he was at a loss for words. All he could think about was how beautiful and perfect she was—and how untouchable. He was beneath her; he knew that even though he had spent the last month and a half telling her that class meant nothing. So why was he so afraid to do what he was longing to do?

"Forgive me, Catherine," he whispered as he captured her lips with his.

He felt her sharp intake of breath as she gasped, but his lips held hers firmly and refused to let her retreat. She tried to lean away but the high back of the chair only allowed her to go so far, and Brant had her pinned firmly against it. She tried to push him away but she didn't have the strength and Brant would not relent. Then he felt her responding. He felt her lips return the embrace and they moved with his just as desperate and hungry as he was. Shocked, he pulled back, but she grabbed him and wouldn't let him leave.

Brant didn't need any more encouragement. He kissed her again, allowing the shock to travel through his entire body. He could tell that Catherine felt it too as she shivered.

When he pulled back this time, she didn't stop him. He searched her face for some kind of indication of how she felt, but she just stared back with big scared eyes and tears streaming down her face.

"What is it?" he asked in concern, reaching out to brush away the salty tears that made tracks down her face.

She brushed him aside and stood up, walking towards the window and turning her back on him.

"Catherine, I'm sorry."

"Please leave."

"I shouldn't have—"

"Leave, Brant!"

He swallowed back his shock and left the cabin. He should never have forced her, never should have taken that next step in their relationship. It wasn't his place and it was deeply inappropriate. She was his passenger; he had rescued her, and was charged with caring for her safety. He shouldn't be putting her in compromising situations. It wasn't as if anything would come of his actions anyway. They were from two different worlds, and those worlds were not meant to mix. All he'd accomplished was complicating things for the last couple of weeks they would have together.

He spent the day working hard, doing small jobs that should have been done by a crew member, anything to keep him busy and not thinking about Catherine. He contemplated eating dinner with the crew instead of with the officers, but decided not to make it look too much like he was avoiding her, so he made an appearance. He had nothing to worry about anyway, Catherine was absent—taking dinner in her cabin.

Sleep was nearly impossible. All he could think about was Catherine and kissing her, kissing those wondrously soft lips and having her respond. He was infatuated and it was interfering with life. It would have been better if he had never taken that step at all. And for the first time, he found himself wishing they had stayed enemies.

* * *

Brant didn't talk to Catherine again until they were nearing the end of their voyage. She had emerged from her cabin the day after the incident, her pride wrapped around her like armor, but she needn't have worried. Brant wasn't about to bother her. He didn't really know why he was doing it but he felt as if, for his own safety, he had to shut her out or he would be lost at sea. Although, he was beginning to think it was already too late for that. He had entered uncharted waters a while ago and now there was no turning back.

He could tell that Karl was concerned about how he was acting, but Brant didn't really care. He had to get away from Catherine. He had to blindfold his eyes, plug his ears, and tie himself to a mast before he threw himself on the rocks to die at the sound of her call. But it wasn't enough. Every time she walked by Brant found himself wanting to be near her. He found himself wanting to talk with her, and walk with her, and sit with her, and he desperately wanted to kiss her again. It was torture. The only way to escape was to lock himself in a cabin, but as captain that wasn't an option. So he suffered through every torturous moment and wished for the day they docked in London to come quickly.

The worst was dinner, now that Catherine was eating with them again. And even though he carefully avoided conversation with her, he could only deflect her for so long.

"Brant, we have to talk."

"I'd rather not, Catherine. I made a mistake."

"I don't want our friendship to suffer because of it."

"It already has. I can't stand to be around you. It takes all my willpower to not kiss you, Catherine. Being around you is torture. Don't wish that upon me."

Catherine sighed and threw up her hands in frustration. "Kiss me then, Brant Foxton! You think I don't want it just as bad?"

Brant looked at her, and when she made no move to retreat or take back what she had said, he took her into his arms and kissed her passionately, all ten days of pent up feelings being set free in one simple act.

He held Catherine tightly against him and rested his chin on the top of her head. "Why do you torture me so?" he whispered, kissing her head.

"I'm sorry, Brant. I'm a selfish woman."

Brant let her go and held her at arm's length. "Catherine, I can't stop this. I can't just wake up tomorrow and decide that I don't care about you. Are you sure about this?"

"No, I'm not. But I'm willing to see what happens. Aren't you?"

Brant nodded, kissing her gently in response. "Let me take you to your cabin. It's late."

* * *

Brant wanted to spend every minute of every remaining day with her. It was a complete turnaround from the last week and a half. They were getting closer to England, and Catherine's home with each passing day, and Brant knew his time with her was limited. He didn't know what he was going to do once they docked, but for now he wanted to make the most of his time with her.

However, work could not fall by the wayside, so he snuck in time with her when he could, and juggled between wanting the day to last forever so that it would take longer to reach England, and wanting evening to come quickly so he could give Catherine his undivided attention. Every evening they would sit in her cabin or in the crow's nest, talking and discussing things much like they had before, but Brant would hold her close, kiss her gently, and brush her hair behind her ears—all the little gestures that showed his feelings beyond friendship.

But, as good as things were going, the day they were only a week away from England came and it came much too soon. When Casper came up to him and announced that weather permitting, and if the wind remained in their favor they would be docking in a week, he found himself almost upset. He hoped a storm would rise up and drive them off course. He hoped that the wind would disappear completely and leave them floating aimlessly; anything to keep the day of Catherine leaving as far away as possible.

They had incredibly smooth sailing the whole two months. Not a storm had arisen, which was strange for this time of year, and the wind had been for the most part in their favor. Nature was conspiring to get Catherine out of his life as quickly as possible. At the beginning of their voyage Brant might have been glad, but so much had changed in a short time and he wasn't ready for it to end. Catherine, on the other hand, seemed to think nothing of it. She remained cheerful and happy, helping Matthew with various activities to help him regain his strength while Brant was busy, and spending every moment with him that he wasn't.

Brant tried to hide how he was feeling and enjoy each moment with her. But he knew she could tell something was bothering him. When he would become silent and distant in the middle of a conversation she would hug him tightly and kiss him on the cheek, whisper for him not to worry and to come back to her. She needed him as much as he needed her. She had a way of making Brant forget about passing time and just enjoy the moment, but the thought of her leaving always returned.

"Brant, you have to stop worrying. You don't know what the future holds," she said one day as he fell into one of his silent moments.

"I'm afraid to find out. I'm not ready for things to change. This is all so new."

She nodded and stroked his face where rough stubble had cropped up in the last couple days. "Just have faith. People do not come together just to be torn apart."

Brant desperately hoped she was right. They deserved to be happy together, didn't they? Catherine was the woman he had always wanted. She was intelligent, brave, strong, and beautiful. She was nothing like the women other men of his profession chose to associate with, she was high class, yet humble and kind. He had always hoped to find someone like her, but thought it impossible. Yet here fate had thrown her at him, and he had to cherish every remaining second with her. To let her go, when he had her in his grasp was too much to ask of a man who had resigned himself to being alone the rest of his life. He couldn't let her go. Not now, not in a week, not ever.

But even though she reassured him there was a reason for this, that they wouldn't be torn apart, he didn't know how he was going to keep her from leaving.

CHAPTER THIRTEEN

As the *BlackFox* sailed into London's port, Brant carefully navigated the ship to a dock. He hadn't seen Catherine all day, and presumed she was packing and getting ready to make an acceptable appearance back into society. As men tied the ship tightly against the dock and lowered the ramp, Catherine finally exited her cabin. She had on a much finer dress than any she had worn since Brant had rescued her. He remembered it though, taken from the clothes he had in the hold, but she hadn't worn it until now. It was a beautiful dark grey, rich with embroidery and a lace collar that went up her neck. She looked elegant, no, regal and Brant felt incredibly uncomfortable in her presence. She had once again adopted the mask and had successfully hidden who she had grown to be in her time on the *BlackFox*.

Approaching her, Brant reached out for an embrace but she recoiled, holding her head up high.

"Not now, Brant."

"Why not?"

"It isn't appropriate. Think how it will look."

Brant frowned but respected her wishes and took a step back. "Is there anything you need out of the cabin?"

She laughed. "I came aboard with nothing. All I have is this," she held up the package of fabric Brant had bought her in Casablanca. She hadn't made use of it yet. "I'm afraid I'm an awful seamstress. I thought I would save it, and have a dressmaker put it to good use."

"And the clothes I gave you?"

"It is all still good. You can make a profit off of it, so I left it all. I just took this dress."

"Then I'll have James fetch a carriage for you."

"Thank you. Will you come with me? I'll have my father pay you."

"Payment really isn't necessary, Catherine."

"I promised you payment. I don't want to bring our relationship into this. Please, accompany me home and I'll have my father give you your due."

Brant nodded. "Very well."

It hurt, how cold Catherine was being. She had reassured him time and again that two people didn't get brought together only to be ripped apart, and yet here she was distancing herself from him in any and every way possible.

He walked off to find James, and once the instructions were given, he went about the many duties that had to be attended to when in a new port. He paid the dock fee, registered his boat, and made arrangements to have his goods looked at by a local merchant. By the time that was all taken care of, a carriage was ready and waiting for them.

He offered Catherine his arm and escorted her down the docks and into the carriage, climbing in and sitting across from her. Brant didn't really know what to say, so he remained quiet for the drive, which proved to be quite short.

The Marshalls lived in a beautiful, ornate townhouse in a rich area near the port. As the carriage pulled to a stop outside their house, Brant hopped out and helped Catherine down, offering his arm to her. She ignored his offered arm, walking past him and up the stairs without so much as a pause at the front door.

Brant watched her in confusion, picked up the package of fabric she had left sitting on the carriage bench, and paid the driver before following her into the house.

He looked around. It was a beautiful house. A black maid, likely a slave, ran down the stairs and stopped in shock. "Miss Catherine!" She turned around and ran back up the stairs shouting out, "Lord Marshall! Lady Marshall!" as she went.

"What is it? What is all this hollering for?" Catherine's father appeared at the top of the stairs looking angry.

She stopped and pointed down the stairs at Catherine. Nothing more had to be said, his anger was obviously forgotten as Lord Marshall's face melted into an expression of shock and joy, and Brant thought maybe a little disbelief. He slowly walked down the stairs, clutching the handrail as if to hold himself upright in his excitement.

"Catherine? Is that you?" He reached out his hand and touched her face as if to ingrain in his mind that she was in fact real and not a figment of his imagination. "You're really here? We heard that your ship was attacked and that there was no sign of you. We thought you were dead."

Catherine embraced her father. "I'm alive, father. Captain Foxton here rescued me."

Lord Marshall reached out his hand to shake Brant's, but didn't let go of Catherine with his other.

A gasp emitted from the top of the stairs, and Catherine's mother ran down, quite unladylike, crying, and embraced her daughter. "You're alive! You're alive!" she sobbed.

Lord Marshall let his daughter go so that his wife could have her moment, and walked over to Brant. "We are forever in your debt, Captain Foxton. If there is anything we can do for you—"

"No, nothing. I was just doing my duty."

"Father, I promised him that we would pay him for my passage."

"It's really quite alright. I didn't do it for the money, sir."

"Nonsense, come with me. You must be paid if that is what you were promised."

Lord Marshall led Brant down a hall and into his study where he opened up a safe and counted out some money. "Does ninety pounds sound fair?"

Brant nodded. "Yes sir. Thank you."

"I really don't know how we can ever repay you. We were told she was gone and had given up hope. You have returned what is most precious to us."

Brant nodded, touched by the obvious love Lord and Lady Marshall had for their daughter, and for a moment even a little jealous he had never had that for himself. "Please, don't trouble yourself. It was a pleasure to aid a lady such as your daughter, and it was nothing beyond my duty as the

King's servant."

"And how long will you be in London?"

"Not long. I hope to set sail within the week if we hope to make it back to Jamaica before the summer storms become bad."

"Then please, join us for dinner tonight. It is the least we can do."

"I would be honored," replied Brant, eager for any excuse to be near Catherine.

* * *

Brant didn't just spend dinner with the Marshalls. He ended up spending the rest of the afternoon with them. He got to meet her younger brother, John (or Johnny as he preferred to be known), who was between boarding schools at the time. He was the same age as James, but a boatload of mischief and trouble; he reminded Brant a lot of himself when he had been that age.

Catherine ignored Brant for the most part. He brushed it off as her not wanting anyone to know about their affair in the last few weeks at sea, but it troubled him slightly. Had it been too much to hope that things wouldn't change between them? She loved him, he was sure, as much as he loved her, but it needed to be said. He would profess his love before he left, and leave it to her to make a decision. She wouldn't leave him, not after everything they had shared and after everything she had said.

So he was charming with her mother, and talked business and politics with her father. No one asked what the purpose of his ship was, and Brant didn't offer an explanation. They all just assumed he was a merchant of some sort and they left it at that.

As dinner approached, Catherine excused herself to get cleaned up, requesting time to take a much needed hot bath after months at sea. Brant and Lord Marshall made their way into the study where they were served whisky and had a drink before dinner was served. An hour later they made their way to the dining room where they joined the women and Johnny.

They were served an incredible meal of turkey, potatoes, fresh vegetables, wine, and fruit… everything anyone could want in a meal. Brant ate until he was full, and then he ate some more. It was all just so good he couldn't bear to let any of it go to waste. Catherine too ate with a vigor that he had never seen in her.

Brant felt at home with Catherine's family. They were kind and gracious to him, and never seemed to look down on him or treat him with contempt. After dinner Lord Marshall excused himself to his study while Johnny went off on his own. Brant was left alone with Catherine and her mother, so he took that as his cue to leave, though he was hesitant to go without having a word in private with Catherine.

"I'm afraid I must take my leave. It is late and I still have much to attend to."

Lady Marshall once again expressed her thanks, and asked Catherine to see him to the door.

"Of course, mother."

Brant stopped in the front entrance and faced Catherine. "I can't leave without speaking with you. Is there somewhere we can talk… alone?"

Catherine frowned. "Outside." She stepped out to the front steps with Brant. "What is it, Brant?"

"I want to be with you, Catherine," he spoke in earnest. "These last few weeks with you have been incredible and I need you in my life. I have a plantation in Jamaica that you could live comfortably on. I'm not a poor man, Catherine."

She shook her head slowly and her eyes welled up with tears. "I can't, Brant."

"What do you mean, you can't?"

"I can't be with you. These last few weeks have been wonderful, yes but they have also been a dream. We can't live like that. You and I are from two different worlds."

"We are not so different. I come from the same world."

"But you chose to leave it. I told you that I could never leave this life, I could never make the same decision you did. Don't ask this of me, Brant."

His brow furrowed and anger coursed through him. What had been all the talk of two people being brought together meaning something? "You made me believe you loved me, you made me fall in love with you. What did you expect, Catherine? That I would just sail away out of your life forever? It doesn't work that way."

"I thought for a moment that I could believe in a fairy tale, Brant," she cried. "But you and I both know fairy tales aren't real and reality has to set in sooner or later. Today is reality."

"Anything can happen if you want it bad enough. Marry me, Catherine. Let me give you a life with me."

"No."

"You will still have all the money and luxury that you enjoy now. Why is this such a terrible thing?"

"Because I can't love a man who will always put the ocean, his ship, before me."

"I love you, Catherine."

"You love the sea more. I'll marry you, Brant, if you give up sailing. Sell the *BlackFox* and give it all up to become a plantation owner. If you do that, then I'll marry you."

Brant looked at her. He felt like he'd been punched in the gut. He would give her the world, but she'd just asked of him the one thing he couldn't give up. "I can't do that."

"Then I can't marry you. I refuse to be second in your life."

"You'd rather marry someone who doesn't love you?"

"I'll marry someone who could give me a real marriage, not someone who would rather be wed to the sea than me. Goodbye, Brant."

Catherine turned on her heel and opened the door, pausing for just a moment to let him see the tears streaming down her face in the soft lantern light, then slammed the door.

He shivered and walked down the steps into the street. He hadn't bothered to fetch a carriage, there were plenty sitting along the side of the road waiting to get a fare, but Brant chose to walk, the cool evening wind helping him forget the pain that Catherine had just inflicted on him. He hadn't expected her to say no. He had thought that perhaps she would take time to think about it, but he had never imagined she would flat out say no and tell him to get out of her life. He thought he had meant more than that to her. He had seen love in her eyes, and she had turned her back on it as easily as choosing one dress over another. Society had once again turned its back on Brant, and he wasn't sure if it was laughing at him for being such a fool, or if it pitied him for thinking he stood a chance with a woman like Catherine.

Walking back on the *BlackFox* Brant locked himself in his cabin, not bothering to respond to any of the crew who said hello as he walked past.

Looking around his cabin he could see remnants of her all around. The book she had been reading was left on his desk. The clothes she had been wearing for the last two months were folded neatly in a corner, and a hand written letter sat on the bed. He picked it up and turned it over in his hand. It likely said everything she had said to him on the steps, but he sat down to read it anyway.

"Dearest Brant,

I hope you understand that I never would want to hurt you, but we cannot be. I have loved these past few months we have spent together, and never has a man treated me with such respect. But our journey has reached its end, and I must leave you.

I made a mistake, falling in love with you, and I am deeply sorry for making you return that love. I assure you that this is no easy decision for me, but I must continue my life here in London as Catherine Marshall, daughter of Lord and Lady Marshall and a member of the royal court. If I were to stay with you, I would need you to give up your life for me. I could not marry a man that would be away from me ten months of the year, and I love you too much to ask you to give up your first love; the ocean. I beg of you to find it in your heart to forgive me. Perhaps our lives will cross paths again.

Always yours,

Catherine Marshall."

Brant read the letter over and over in an attempt to understand, to allow it to sink in that she had left him and she was not coming back. He had heard it from her own mouth, and now he had it in writing, yet he couldn't quite believe that she would be so willing to give up.

* * *

Brant buried himself in work for the next couple of days. He sold his cargo and bought more supplies, and now it was time to cast off and head home for the summer. Matthew approached him as he was charting a course with Casper.

"Sir, I would like to stay aboard if that's okay."

Brant looked up at the fifteen year old boy and smiled. "Of course. You will work under Casper."

"Thank you, sir."

"Welcome to the crew, Matthew."

Brant climbed up to the crow's nest to bid London goodbye as they sailed away. He could imagine that Catherine was standing somewhere along the docks waving her last goodbyes to him, but he doubted it. She had already said her goodbyes, and now it was his turn to say his.

Watching London disappear slowly, he turned to face the open ocean. It was a beautiful thing to see nothing but waves and blue sky ahead and not really knowing what lay beyond the distant horizon. The ocean was a mystery to Brant, but it captured his imagination and held him enthralled for eight years of his life.

Brant pulled Catherine's letter out of his pocket and read it over one last time, then let it go, flying in the wind until it landed somewhere among the white tipped waves.

When London was out of sight Brant climbed down and went to join the crew for dinner. The usual joy was missing from his demeanor, and he couldn't find it in him to joke. Instead he ate in silence, and watched as men all around him laughed. They were happy with their life, and for the first time in seven years Brant was not. He watched James and Matthew talk together like brothers, and he smiled slightly, but still could find very little joy in the sight of his brother finding a friend.

He left dinner, his food only half eaten, and made his way into the hold where he pulled out a dusty bottle of rum. Walking on deck, he uncorked it and took a long drink. The rum burned down his throat and sat warmly in his core. It helped him forget the sight, sound, smell, and even taste of her, of his love. Taking another long swig, he sat down against the rail and cried. He cried for his mother, his lost childhood, his father, his brother, for Catherine, and for himself. He cried for the lives that he had taken, and he cried for the families that would miss them. He cried because there was nothing left to do but to let years of pent up sorrow free.

He heard footsteps, and he quickly wiped the tears away and looked up to see who would dare disturb his private moment of despair. Karl sat down beside him and reached out his hand for the bottle.

"Been a strange couple months, ain't it?"

Brant nodded. "That it has."

"And that Catherine, she be gone now."

"Yes. She's home."

"You gonna miss her?"

Brant laughed bitterly. "What kind of question is that, Karl?"

"Just a question."

"You and every man on the crew knew what was going on, and you ask me if I miss her?"

"You shouldn't have let it happen, Brant."

"You're a little late to give that advice."

"Yer a grown man. You should have known it couldn't go nowhere good. She don't belong in your world, and you sure don't belong in hers."

"Don't lecture me about where I belong."

"Yer looking like you need it. I'm seeing you go down a dark path because of a woman and I won't abide for that. Now you need to mourn, then so be it. Cry away because it takes more of a man to admit to his pain than to hide from it. It's a healing thing. But don't you dare let this ship suffer because you went on a foolhardy chase after some noble woman."

"I loved her, Karl."

"I don't doubt it, but you didn't love her enough. Not to give her what she deserved. If I see you going down a dark place, Brant, I swear I gonna hit you hard. Don't you forget that."

Brant nodded and held out his hand for the bottle. Karl handed it back to him after he took a swig, and Brant took a long drink. "Am I to spend my whole life alone?"

"We all do. Tis cause we already gave our life to the ocean. Me, the crew, this ship, even you... no woman will take us, cause they can't own us, we've already given our hearts to the sea."

Brant sighed and nodded. Getting up, he threw the bottle overboard. "I'm not going to be better overnight, Karl."

"Aye."

Brant walked away, but looked one last time out to the dark waters. Life would go on even though Catherine was gone. Days would be darker for a time, but Brant would crawl out of the hole and become his old self once again, resigned to being alone. But until that day came he would hurt. He would hurt every day until the image of a tall blonde woman standing up on the crow's nest with her hair blowing in the wind was permanently erased from his mind. But when the day came that she was gone the ocean could have him; heart and soul.

PLEASE ENJOY AN EXCERPT FROM
BOOK 1 OF THE OCEAN SERIES:
HEART LIKE AN OCEAN

HEART LIKE AN OCEAN

PROLOGUE

Spain-1666

Senona looked around the room full of swirling dresses of so many shapes and colors. It was like a dream and left her overwhelmed and unable to tear her eyes away. Tonight she was a princess in her new dress with her hair curled, cascading in loose waves down her back. Tonight she was perfect.

Browsing the room, this time in search of familiar faces, Senona spotted Caton Amador, and Isidro Amato. The boys, although older, were her friends and a welcome relief to the overwhelming nature of her surroundings. She made her way around the perimeter of the room in their general direction.

Isidro was never very serious about anything and enjoyed teasing Senona, which annoyed her to no end. Caton was much more subdued and quiet, at least around her. Although they were not as close as they once had been, the families remained good friends, and the three of them spent many hours riding around the countryside or playing games in the garden. When they were younger, Isidro and Caton had been her constant companions, helping her sneak out of tea with their Madres or rescuing her from lessons with her tutor. Now they never voluntarily saw each other, but due to their families' relationship, they found themselves together often enough.

"Senona, my Chica! You are a picture of beauty, as always," boomed Isidro's obnoxious and teasing voice.

Caton turned to look at the young girl. "Leave her alone, Isidro."

"Come on, Caton. She's glad to see us."

Caton frowned but said nothing, turning his attention back to the pretty girl standing next to him. Isidro seemed to accept that as permission to continue, and he smirked mockingly at Senona, beckoning her. The small flock of girls that surrounded the two boys giggled, causing her to blush and become hesitant and uncomfortable. She had never seen the boys in this environment, and she quickly questioned her decision that she belonged with them.

"It's okay, Isidro. I just wanted to say hello."

"Well then, run along. There must be some of your friends around."

Senona forced a smile and turned to Caton. "Hello, Caton."

He barely acknowledged her with a brief glance and nod in her direction, and then returned to ignoring her. Unsure of how to deal with Caton's rejection, she walked away, her eyes burning with angry tears that threatened to spill over. Why was he being so rude? Not even so much as a hello, as if he were embarrassed to be associated with her.

As she pushed her way through the crowd, she heard one of the girls laugh. "Caton, I do believe you hurt her feelings."

Caton's deep, unmistakable chuckle cut through the din and his voice was all she heard. "She's a silly, strange girl. I would rather not encourage her."

Senona expected this behavior from Isidro, but from Caton? She had always thought he was honest and simple, but his actions tonight had shown her otherwise. She had been a fool to think that these older boys were her friends.

Escaping into the shadows, she hid from the sneering glances and mocking laughter that seemed to follow her wherever she went. She had thought that tonight would be different, but nothing had changed. She was just a strange little girl.

The night was a blur, a blur of swirling skirts and obnoxious voices. To nearly everyone she was invisible. Even her Madre and Padre, who had never been overly affectionate towards their daughter, seemed to have completely forgotten her existence. But that wasn't so different from normal. They weren't very affectionate people ever, even towards each other.

At the end of the night, Senona lay in bed, her new dress hanging in her wardrobe, mocking her. She had realised tonight how far she fell from society's standards, her own parents' standards. Any illusion she had of being a princess, of being perfect for one night had been shattered. But that didn't really bother her. The truly odd thing was that she felt a weight lifted from her shoulders. Perhaps she didn't have to be that way. Perhaps now she had the freedom to do as she wanted. It wasn't as if anyone cared about her anyway. She was just a strange little girl.

CHAPTER ONE

Three years later Spain-1669

Senona looked back hesitantly as she entered the dark stable where her father's horses were kept. It was the middle of the night; the countryside was quiet as slumber had overtaken everyone and everything around. She was confident that no one had witnessed her escape from the manor, nor would anyone know of her disappearance until morning. That was how she intended it; let them find out the bride had run the night before her wedding. She wouldn't allow herself to become the trophy wife of an arranged marriage.

She was young, though not so young that she shouldn't already be married. Nearing her twenties, she could have married anytime within the last three years, though she'd found no suitable match. Being the daughter of Don Marco Montez meant she would not marry just anyone, and her parents' final decision was with an older, rich, and influential Doctor from Barcelona, Senor Flamez.

Senor Flamez was nearing fifty and widowed not five years earlier. She was to be his second wife, more to help him run his dilapidated household than anything else. Rumor had it that Senor Flamez had allowed things to fall apart after Senora Flamez passed away in childbirth, losing the child along with her. It would be Senona's job to make the man happy again, provide him with an heir and allow his life to become what it had been in previous years: rich, elegant, and prestigious. How he came to the conclusion that she would be suitable for that role she could not fathom.

Senona was not, by any definition, elegant or humble. She was quick to anger and didn't much enjoy doing the domestic duties expected of a good wife. Instead, she could be more often than not found in a pasture or riding along the high cliffs bordering the coast of the Mediterranean Sea. Perhaps that was why her Madre and Padre were so pleased to have found her a husband; she would no longer be their problem or embarrassment.

This late at night the horses made very little noise. A few stamped their hooves or rustled the hay; otherwise, the only sound was their breathing. Senona's horse was a young stallion; a Spanish horse with the best pedigree money could buy. He had been a gift for her sixteenth birthday. Only a young colt then, she had trained him herself and preferred no other horse in her father's stable over Naldo.

Saddling him quickly and quietly, she shoved the small amount of clothes she had carried from her room into a saddlebag. She hid a bag of doubloons, which she had stolen from her father's safe, carefully among them. It was a small fortune and would surely have her father's hounds chasing her as soon as the red sun rose above the horizon. However, she did not plan to be on land by then. She would find a ship where she would be much harder to track. Perhaps, like the romantic stories, she would be able to disappear into the horizon never to be seen again. One could only hope. Yet, as she mounted Naldo and rode him down the road that led to Barcelona, Senona found herself looking back in sadness. Although she had not been happy here, it was her home and this would be the last time she'd ever see it. No longer would she be living the life of comfort that she was accustomed to, no longer would she be secure in her future, and no longer would she be able to wake up every morning without fear or worry. Was she truly ready for this life? Looking forward again she refused to allow herself another glance back. Whether she was ready for this change or not, she had made up her mind, and she would go through with it. As hard and as treacherous as it may be, wasn't freedom worth it?

Upon first entering Barcelona, the streets were quiet and abandoned. Rich homes and rich families resided here, and they were all in bed at this late hour. However, as she drew closer to the docks, she came across more and more people, none looking very reputable, many giving her looks that made her uneasy. There were still a few safe places near the docks though. The merchant's quarter housed many rich men, friends of her parents, the Amadors, being only one of them. Senona missed the years when she had been friends with Caton Amador. Age changed things and people, and as a result, friendships slipped away.

Not really knowing where to start, only knowing what her destination was to be, Senona dismounted and led Naldo to the docks in hope that a

Captain would be around from whom she could buy passage to Port Royale. There, in a British colony, she would be out of her parents' reach. She could start a new life.

While the rest of Barcelona was very much asleep, the docks were alive with activity. Music and raucous voices came from the many taverns that lined the docks, all dangerous places that Senor Amador had warned her about many times when taking her on tours of his ships. This was no place for a lady at any time of day, much less in the middle of the night. But desperate times called for desperate measures, and she was certain there would be more than a few Captains in these taverns ready and willing to make some extra gold. Finding one who would willingly enter British waters would be a little harder. Pirates and privateers patrolled there, and it'd be even harder to find one who would allow a horse onboard. The few who would have allowed Naldo held to the old sailor's superstition that having a woman aboard would bring bad luck. This made the task of finding passage more difficult than Senona had expected. Only one Captain, an Englishman, Old Richard, seemed to hold no qualms.

"Port Royale ye say?"

"Si, Senor, are you making port there at all?"

"Just so happens I is. It will cost ye though. It's bad luck for a woman to be onboard, and I ain't too fond of livestock."

"How much?" It was never a question of the money to Senona. It was her Padre's, and its only purpose to her was to get her far away.

"Fifty pieces of eight."

Senona nodded. "And when do you leave?" "First light."

"I'll give you thirty doubloons to cast off within the next two hours."

"Two hours, eh? I ain't barely supplied."

"Stop at the next port and get your supplies then. I can take my money elsewhere." Senona spoke with authority and confidence that she did not feel. She had seen her Padre conduct business and knew that if she was to get her way, she had to appear in control. She carefully placed the bag of doubloons on the dirty wood table to illustrate she was able to provide what she promised. Old Richard's eyes gleamed greedily.

"Aye, two hours and the *Sea Vulture* shall cast off."

"I shall see you then, Captain." She got up and reached for the bag but Old Richard grabbed her wrist. Her eyes narrowed, but she held herself in check. She was in a strange place right now, and it wasn't a good idea to start any trouble.

"I'll be needing that pay in advance."

Senona smiled, gently pulling her hand from his grip and counted out the promised coins. "Two hours, Captain. I cannot wait longer than that."

Senona walked away, leaving the smoky, loud tavern behind a closed door and breathed in the fresh sea air. Naldo was tied to a hitching post only a few feet away, nickering softly in greeting. There was something about that man that made her uneasy, but she was left with little choice. Therefore, as unpleasant as this voyage was going to be, she would have to make the best of it.

In a far corner of the bar, hidden by shadows that the lanterns and candles didn't quite reach, a man got up and followed the girl out into the dark night. He was tall and moved smoothly from years of practice at walking on rolling ship decks. A brace of pistols and a long cutlass were strapped to his belt.

He had not been blind to the transaction that had occurred between the girl and Old Richard, nor was he oblivious, as she seemed to be, of the danger she was in.

Following her at a safe distance, he waited to see what she would do. There were only a few short hours before she would find out that she had not bought passage but instead sold herself into the white slave market, of which there was plenty of demand and good return. Old Richard was no fool. He had seen how naïve this girl was, and he immediately saw the profit he could make. She had been sheltered, it was apparent by her trust in humanity. Stupid girl, foolish girl. It would serve her right if he just allowed her to continue on her self-destructive path. She thought her life was hard now? Just wait until she started her new life, the life Old Richard chose for her. He couldn't allow it though. For all his questionable morals, Brant Foxton could not, with clear conscience, allow this girl to fall into the hands of Old Richard.

The girl had led her horse down the docks a little way, but now she chose to stop. Looking around she sat down, looking ready to wait for the next two hours. He studied her and sighed. He was sure he would not be able to trick her into coming onto his ship instead of Old Richard's, nor would she be so trusting as to accept passage for free. That would raise red flags in her mind. She was not stupid, merely sheltered.

Watching her a while, he became certain she wouldn't leave. He had less than two hours to get his crew together and leave town. Turning, he left the girl and her horse and walked the short distance to where his ship sat docked. Most of his crew would be away from ship. He had promised them a two day leave and they would be enjoying it. The only souls aboard the *BlackFox* would be Karl and Matt, taking care of tonight's watch, and James, the cabin boy, who was likely sleeping soundly below deck. But even with the four of them, that was not enough to sail a ship of the *BlackFox's* size, nor enough to successfully kidnap a girl at the same time.

Walking aboard, Matt, a young sailor who had been with him for the past three years greeted him. He had proven himself honest, hardworking, and exceptionally skilled as a sailor and had quickly worked his way through the ranks. Matt was the sailing master and a damn good one. If Karl ever decided to retire, which was unlikely, he was set to take his place as Quartermaster. For now, Brant took advantage of Matt's exceptional navigation skills.

"Top of the evening to ye, Cap'n."

"That it is, Matthew. I need you to do something for me."

Matt, who was sitting near the mast playing a guitar, stopped and nodded. "Yes, sir?"

"There's a bit of trouble brewing, and I need you to collect the crew. We need to set sail as soon as possible."

"Militia?"

"No, just some trouble with another Captain. Tell anyone who won't come that he'll have to find a new billet. I wait for no man."

"Yes, sir." Matt took off without another word. "Karl!"

An older man stood up by the railing of the upper deck. He stood unsteadily, visibly leaning on the railing for support. "Brant, there'd better be a damned good reason why you're hollering at me at this time of night," he slurred.

"Karl, is there a reason you're yelling at your Captain?"

The man slowly made his way down the stairs and approached him. Standing closer than was comfortable, Brant could smell the rum on his breath. "Brant Foxton, you may be Captain but I raised ye from when ye were naught but knee high. I'll talk to ye however I wish when the crew ain't around to bear witness."

Brant laughed and took a slight step back. "We're leaving in a couple of hours. When the crew arrives, I need you to make sure things are ready to set sail. I have an errand to run."

"Aye, Brant. Trouble?"

"Nothing to be too worried about, I would just rather not be in port come morning. Go sober up; there's some coffee in the galley."

Karl walked off somewhat unsteadily to the galley. Brant sighed. James would be asleep in the crew's quarters. He would rather he stayed asleep till morning, but someone had to get together a makeshift stall and collect enough water to make the next port. The rest of their supplies would be collected then. As for the crew, if he could find a handful sober enough to function, things might just work out.

The crew began to stagger in about twenty minutes later, all drunk and grumbling unhappily about their festivities being cut short. However, as unhappy as they were, they were all there within the hour. Not a man was missing. Walking among them, Brant instructed them all to get some hot coffee from the galley. Only Matt and the master gunner, Christopher, were sober enough to help him with the more delicate task of getting the girl aboard.

"You two, come with me," he instructed.

The girl still sat where Brant had left her only an hour earlier. Her horse stirred slightly but seemed content to stand watch near his mistress.

"Forgive me, Cap'n, but since when are we in the kidnapping business? This don't sit well with me," said Matt nervously.

"Matthew, we're immoral men. If you're choosing now to grow a conscience, perhaps you should find another line of work."

Neither man responded.

"I don't care if you two have to bind and gag the girl, just get her to the ship in one piece and preferably unharmed. I'll look after the horse."

"Yes, sir," they chorused.

Brant stood back as the two men approached the girl. It pained him to see the look of surprise and then terror cross over the girl's face as Christopher grabbed her from behind. She dropped the horse's lead rope as she struggled to break free, but Matt made quick work of tying her up and then there was very little she could do. They were efficient; he could say that much. No scream managed to escape her lips, and although she struggled as Matt carried her over his shoulder, he never once faltered.

Brant went over to the startled horse that was dancing in confusion and picked up the forgotten lead rope. He followed behind them at a distance, being careful that the girl didn't see his face. He didn't need her recognizing him when morning came and explanations had to be made. Christopher fell into stride with Brant as they approached the ship.

"Where would ye like her, Cap'n?"

"Put her in my cabin for now. I don't imagine I'll need it tonight."

It would be a long night. With the majority of his crew drunk, he could only hope Old Richard didn't figure out who interfered until morning. All that aside, Brant would be happy if his stumbling, useless crew managed to get his ship out of the harbor unscathed.

A rough hand clamped over her mouth silenced Senona's scream. Her muffled protests brought no sympathy or release from either of the men. For only a brief second, his hand left her face, but he quickly replaced it with a musty, salty tasting gag. The other man picked her up easily, slinging her uncomfortably over his shoulder, as if she were a sack of flour. Though she struggled against her captor, Senona couldn't see where she was going; only the retreating view of where she had been sitting a moment ago and a dark figure followed with Naldo.

They walked up a long, wooden plank. So they were taking her aboard a ship. She had heard of young girls being kidnapped and sold as slaves. Was that to be her sad fate? However, much to her surprise, she heard the man who had been following instruct for her to be put in his cabin, not the brig as she had expected.

Upon entering the cabin, the man gently lowered her to the floor.

"I'm quite sorry, ma'am. I ain't in the business of kidnapping but orders is orders."

He removed her gag slowly but replaced it with his rough hand, once again cutting off her screams. "Now I know you wanna scream and all, but no one here is gonna help. So it would be mightily appreciated if you'd just keep quiet and save up all that screaming for the Cap'n. Lord knows he deserves it."

Senona wanted to ask what they would do with her and what they had done with Naldo, but she found herself too terrified to speak. Panic coursed through her body leaving her trembling against the man's hand. How did she manage to get herself into such a situation?

The man left her alone in the dark cabin. Closing the door behind him, she heard the distinct click of a lock.

Getting up slowly, she stumbled to the wall and felt her way around the room until she found a bed. She was exhausted and scared. All she wanted was to feel the warmth and comfort of a bed. She had an overwhelming urge to cry, but tears wouldn't fall. She was just too tired for tears, too tired to think about what had happened in the short time since she had left home, too tired to even function. Answers would have to wait till morning.

When Senona awoke the next morning, she was greeted by the sight of a young man with short blonde hair, sitting with an air of superiority. He was intently studying a map laid out on the ornate desk situated in the center of the room.

"Welcome to the land of the living," said the man, without so much as a glance up from his map .

"Senor, may I ask where the Captain is?" she asked. "Captain Brant Foxton at your service," he said with a smirk, this time rewarding her with his undivided attention.

Standing up, she drew herself to her full height. "So you are the man responsible for my abduction. What do you plan to do with me, Captain? Sell me as a slave? And where is my horse? You owe me an explanation for how I was treated last night."

She squared her five-foot-five body, waiting for his response. She could see him looking her over and his lips pressed together in a smirk.

"Yes, yes you would bring me a tidy sum on the black market. I know a few men off Tortuga who would be more than willing to take you, but that is not what I have in mind. Old Richard, however, the 'oh so kind' Captain whom you purchased passage from had just that in mind. He is most likely sitting in Barcelona right now very upset that the young Senorita did not show up. Though I am sure he has spent your doubloons quite frivolously already. Aside from that, I can assure you that your stallion is safe and content below deck."

"Captain Richard and I had a business deal. I don't know what made you think his intentions were anything less than pure when you are much more suspicious in my mind. Only the most diabolical man abducts and that is-" Brant cut her off sharply. "Stop right there, Miss. I am a man of honor, which may be hard for you to believe seeing as what I put you through last night, but I will not have my character questioned by a girl who has barely seen eighteen years and hasn't sullied her ears with even the maid's gossip. Old Richard would never have brought you to Port Royale. I will. That is a fact and I urge you to accept it."

"I don't see what else I can do given the present circumstances. However, I cannot afford to pay you. I'm afraid you have brought any costs and trouble I bring upon your own head." She could afford to pay him, and she was certain he knew that, but since he had forcibly taken her aboard his ship, Senona had decided that it would be at his cost, not hers.

"Don't worry over the cost. We will hardly notice you. I can't guarantee a direct course to Port Royale, as I have other, paying business, to attend to. We can discuss this all later tonight though. You will join me for dinner." There was no room for argument in his voice.

"Of course, Captain," she spat out snidely, knowing there was no use in protesting. The man seemed trustworthy enough--for someone that had just kidnapped her--and her energy was better spent elsewhere than fighting a useless battle.

"Wonderful. You are free to wander around the ship as you please, but try to stay out of the way. This is your cabin to use for the remainder of the voyage; however, I will have to make use of it from time to time as all my things are here. Now if you'll excuse me I have a lot of things to attend to. We left in such a great hurry last night, and I can't say any of my crew is overly pleased. We will likely be making port in the next few days to stock up. You have until then to decide if you wish to stay aboard the *BlackFox*. I assure you that you will not be kept here against your will." Bowing slightly, he left the cabin, giving her a brief glimpse of a clear, blue sky through the open door.

Senona sighed and fell back down on the bed, grimacing as her head hit harder than she'd expected. Sitting up again, she looked around. The cabin was bare except for the large desk and dresser. There were no portraits or items of sentiment. No clues as to who the young Captain was. The only thing that gave Senona an insight into his character was the ornate woodwork that gave testimony to expensive and sophisticated taste. He was no simple Captain, of that Senona was certain.

Straightening her dress and quickly braiding her long hair, Senona left the cabin to explore her surroundings and find Naldo. The ship wasn't large, obviously not meant for passengers, but instead for speed. Below deck, Naldo was calmly eating some hay. The fact that he was in a dark and smelly ship hold didn't seem to faze him at all. "Good morning, Naldo. I hope your night went better than mine." She stroked his muscled shoulder rhythmically as she spoke.

"He slept well, ma'am. I found him stretched right out on the floor when I came down to feed him this morning. Good thing I made the stall big so he could rest his legs," said a young version of the Captain, as he came down the steps with a large pail of water in hand; he looked to be about sixteen.

"Yes, very thoughtful of you. How long do you suppose the supply of water and hay will last?"

"Only a few days. We'll make Port Gibraltar by the end of the week and get more. We left in a bit of a hurry last night."

"Thank you for looking after Naldo for me. What is your name?"

"James Foxton," he responded, not offering any further information. "Just doing my job, ma'am."

Senona smiled as she watched James walk away cheerfully. The Captain was a mystery. She didn't understand how the same man who ordered her abduction could also have such a happy boy on his crew, a boy that she was certain was his younger brother. She picked some clean straw off the floor of Naldo's stall and gave him a quick brushing. Finding his halter and lead rope dumped unceremoniously on a crate, she put them on Naldo, who nuzzled her as she did so.

"Come, Naldo, let's get your legs stretched."

Senona didn't know why she always spoke to him. She knew he couldn't understand her, but somehow, it gave her an odd sort of comfort that someone was listening, even if it was only a horse. She led him out of his stall and up on deck. He followed her calmly, but his eyes showed his apprehension towards his new surroundings, and his ears twitched in constant attention. The sailors going about their various jobs and the surrounding water alarmed Naldo, but he stayed close to Senona, her reassuring words helping to calm him.

"That's a fine looking stallion ye got there."

Senona gave a start and turned around to face a grizzled, yet kind faced old man. He wore a large smile that, she suspected, could put even her Padre at ease. "Thank you."

"The name's Karl. I'm the Quartermaster here."

"Senona Montez."

"Pleased to meet ye. If any of the crew gives ye any trouble, ye come see me. We ain't too used to guests."

"I'll try to stay out of the way."

"Don't ye worry your pretty little head about that. No one is gonna mind. I'm just makin' sure the men here treat ye right." Karl turned to walk away but Senona stopped him.

"Karl?"

"Yes, my pretty?"

"Why does the Captain keep James aboard? How does he get his education?"

"We're naught but simple sailors. How would the Cap'n accomplish that? Educations are for rich people, men much better than us."

"There is more to the Captain and his brother than this life."

"Ye can keep those ideas if ye like, but I ain't gonna confirm them. The boy is happy here and, although this life is a hard one, even I can't say he'd be better off on shore. The Cap'n does his best to do right by him."

"Are there no parents?"

"Begging your pardon, miss, but I can't be answering questions about neither the Captain nor his brother. You're just gonna have to ask him yourself."

"Thank you, Karl."

"Aye."

Karl walked away, leaving Senona alone in the middle of a deck crawling with activity. Making her way over to the railing where she hoped to be out of the way, she leaned out to try and catch a glimpse of Barcelona. It was there; a dark line along the horizon. She could just make out the cliffs that she had ridden across so many times.

"You seem to have the young stallion's trust. Not many horses would be so calm at sea," said Brant as he approached her.

"Naldo has trust in me, and that was not easy to earn. But as calm as he looks, he is quite nervous."

"I wouldn't guess it."

"Not everything is as it seems. See, his eyes are wide and anxious, his ears are constantly moving in total attention, and if you touch him, you will feel that he is trembling. If not for his complete trust in me, Naldo would flee."

"I was raised in a lord's house and had riding instructors of the best caliber but none ever taught me this," said Brant thoughtfully, as he studied

Naldo more closely. "It's as if he's talking to you with every move he makes."

Senona smiled, so she had guessed right that he was a noble.

"That is exactly what he's doing. Teachers tell you how to handle a horse, how to tame it, and be master over it. They do not teach you how to communicate or form a partnership with one."

"You're different from other noblewomen I've known."

"I certainly hope so. If you hadn't been able to see any difference, I would have been insulted."

Brant put her at ease. It was an uncommon feeling for her as she was used to constantly being on edge around people. What made it even stranger was that this man should terrify and anger her. He had taken her aboard his ship against her will, and now she found herself talking to him as if he were a friend, something she hadn't had in quite some time.

"I knew you were a noble from the moment I saw you, but there was something in your demeanor that made it apparent that you are different." Then he added, "Besides, what woman would leave a home such as the Montez estate?"

"Then you know who I am."

Brant's eyes sparkled in silent amusement. "Well, rumors do get around with the young women about 'that Montez girl.' I'm afraid I'd recognize you almost anywhere. Aren't you missing your wedding today?"

"I am. I'm sure I will be the scandal of the season after this exploit." She laughed. "I'll leave you to your work though. I think Naldo has had quite enough fresh air."

After making sure Naldo was comfortable and had everything he needed, Senona went back on deck. Still unsure of what to make of the situation she found herself in, she figured the best thing to do was to keep busy and keep her mind off of things until a decision had to be made.

Due to the ship leaving in such a hurry, there was plenty that needed doing. Karl was walking around the deck giving orders to men or inspecting their work. He seemed to be a gentle task master. Senona observed him dealing with a few younger sailors and was surprised to see him carefully explain what they had done incorrectly and proceed to show them how it was to be done. Not once did she hear an angry word cross his lips. As he passed near Senona, she called him over. "Karl, is there anything I can do?"

Karl stopped and looked at her, surprised. "Have ye ever been on a ship?"

"No, but I'm a fast learner."

He looked thoughtful. "Well, I ain't got time to show ye much now, but perhaps ye can take a climb up to the crow's nest. Take a good look around and let me know what ye see."

Senona glanced down at her skirt and was all the more thankful that she'd worn a simple dress without the layers and layers of petticoats that would have impeded her climb. With a nod of her head and a shrug of her shoulders, Senona walked off towards the mast and was climbing quickly up the small ladder before Karl could get another word in. The thought of anyone being able to see up her skirts barely crossed her mind. She'd been climbing trees all her life and modesty was not something she had ever worried much about, plus it gave her a smug sense of satisfaction to imagine her mother's face if she could see her now.

Senona had never been so high in her life, and the view did not disappoint. It was breathtaking. She looked around and saw the thin lines that were the land masses of Spain and Africa on either side. However, out here in middle of the Mediterranean Sea they were completely alone with nothing but the wind and the waves for company, friends that could quickly turn on you out in open water. It was a daunting thought, being at the mercy of the waves and on a less than reputable ship. She had seen the Jolly Roger hanging idly below. Captain Foxton made no effort to hide his ship's purpose.

She could have climbed down then and reported to Karl, but instead she chose to enjoy the view.

"Breathtaking, ain't it?" asked a young man, standing on the spar directly below her.

Senona guessed he had just finished unfurling a sail, though she was too caught up in her own thoughts to notice. Reaching down, she held her skirts tightly against her legs, something she hadn't been able to do while climbing.

"It's amazing. I would almost be content to stay here forever."

"Almost, but not quite?" asked the man.

"Not quite. There is something about solid ground under your feet that you just can't replace. You're at the mercy of the wind and water here. At least on land you have more control. My name's Senona."

"Matt."

Senona smiled. She had yet to receive an introduction that included a last name from anyone besides the Captain and his brother. "It's nice to meet you, Matt. If you don't mind me asking, what is life like on this ship?" It wouldn't hurt to try and get an idea of what the Captain was like, and what better way to do so than to find out from the men who spent every day with him?

"Best life I ever had. The Cap'n looks after his crew better than most Cap'ns. Don't base what ye think of him by what happened last night. He's a good man."

"That's hard to believe."

"Ye aren't angry with me. I was the one that hauled ye here."

Senona grimaced. She had thought he sounded familiar but hadn't wanted to make any accusations. It wouldn't have gotten her anywhere to cause conflict. "On his orders."

"He was trying to help ye."

She said nothing. Could she really deny that? There had been no evidence to the contrary, and she had to admit they were treating her quite admirably so far, aside from the previous night.

Matt smiled a cocky sort of grin. He knew she had no argument. "I best be getting down. Karl will be hollering up at me soon to get down and back to work." He made his way over to a shroud and began to shimmy down.

Senona took one last look around and then she too climbed down to inform Karl of how alone they were. But with the threat of land all around her, Senona felt they weren't alone enough. She was still too close to home to be safe.

Senona walked into the Captain's dining room that night wearing the same clothes she had worn the night before, and all day. It was very much against her upbringing, but she had a limited supply of clothing. She blushed briefly upon realising she was late and had caused the Captain, Karl, and James to wait. However, she quickly shook it off. After all, she was among pirates, not among the nobility of Spain.

"Good evening," she said with a forced smile.

Brant stood up and helped Senona to her seat, directly to the right of his.

"Thank you, Captain," she said, sitting quietly and placing a napkin on her lap.

The array of food was spectacular, considering they were on a ship, and one that had left in a hurry at that. Senona thought back to the days when she had been friends with Caton; he had told her horror stories about the food on ships and was somewhat relieved to see they weren't true.

"This all looks quite amazing, Captain."

"This is only the first day at sea. Just wait until we've been out here for a few weeks. Not much will look good then," said James.

Brant chuckled. "I'm afraid he's right. I would recommend enjoying it while the food is still fresh. We are fortunate that the cook had the good sense to get a few things when we had first docked."

At this, everyone started to eat. Those few words seemed to instill haste in everyone, as if the food may go stale as they sat there. However, after a few minutes of eating in silence, Senona spoke up, not entirely comfortable with the lack of conversation.

"How long do you expect to be at sea before we dock in Port Royale?" she asked between mouthfuls of potatoes.

Brant lifted an eyebrow in amusement. "You're staying with your kidnappers then?"

"I haven't decided yet, but I thought it best to make an informed decision."

"It all depends on the weather, how many enemy ships we come across, and how often we make port. I'd say maybe two or three months. I try to stay out the entire season if possible."

"Do you come across enemy ships often?" Senona asked, knowing very well they weren't enemy ships at all, just ships ripe for picking by pirates like Brant Foxton. This was no military vessel.

"Yes, ma'am, the French and Dutch have become quite bold, and the Spanish, well, we like them the best," informed James. Brant winced and kicked him under the table.

James gave Brant a glare that no cabin boy should get away with while Senona studied the whole exchange in fascination. Smiling, she replied, "Let's not ignore the purpose of this ship. I'm not completely ignorant."

Karl smiled, but remained silent as the other three spoke. He didn't seem to feel any need to speak while he was enjoying his food whole-heartedly.

Brant, however, did not seem comfortable with the subject they had breached and quickly changed it. "How do you think Naldo will do? Three months is a long time for a horse to be cooped up."

"I can't really say. If I find he's taking it badly, I suppose I'll just have to get off when we make port. If I stay, that is."

"The horse'll do fine," reassured Karl.

"You're sure?" asked Senona.

"Horses get transported by ship all the time in war or to the colonies. He'll do just fine after he's had some time to get used to everything."

"I hope you're right, Karl. Whether on this ship or another, I would like to get all the way to Port Royale."

Brant stood up then. His plate had been completely polished off. "If you will all excuse me, I believe I'm going to turn in for the night."

"G'night, Cap'n," said Karl.

"Lessons first thing in the morning, James," said Brant sternly.

James scowled a little but nodded his assent, and on that note, Brant left the room.

Karl followed Brant's example not much later. "My old age don't allow me many late nights anymore," he explained with a smile before he too took his leave to make one last round of the ship.

"Will you come with me to check on Naldo?" Senona asked James.

"Of course."

The two of them went below deck, laughing as they went, with James telling Senona some of the more amusing stories of things that had happened on the ship.

When she had woken up that morning, she had been scared, confused, and angry. She had been on a strange ship with strange people and, in the span of a single day, the crew had made her feel happy and at home. That was something Senona was only now experiencing for the first time in her life.

Available now in print and digital.

ABOUT THE AUTHOR

Christine Steendam is the award-winning romance author of the Foremost Chronicles and the Ocean Series.

Christine Makes her home in Manitoba, Canada on a sprawling 15 acre ranch with her husband, two young sons, and a brood of animals including Guinness, her beloved chocolate quarter horse.

www.christinesteendam.com

www.ingramcontent.com/pod-product-compliance
Lightning Source LLC
Chambersburg PA
CBHW072356190626
46811CB00019B/942